What the Critics are Say
H. J. Ralles' Novels

Keeper of the Kingdom

"Aimed at young adults, this is ingenious enough to appeal powerfully to adults who wonder how far this entire computer age can go. Ralles knows how to pace her story—the action moves in sharp chase-and-destroy scenes as Commanders hunt down the dangerous young boy. The pages literally brim with action and computer possibilities and discoveries. The characters are memorable, particularly the very human 101. And that ending . . . is brilliant. A compelling read from exciting beginning to just as exciting ending." *The Book Reader*

"*Keeper of the Kingdom* is a must read for children interested in computers and computer games. From the first page to the last there is no relief from the suspense and tension. H. J. Ralles has captivated anyone with a fascination for computer games, and has found a way to connect computer-literate children to reading." **JoAn Martin,** *Review of Texas Books*

"*Keeper of the Kingdom* is a fun read for younger readers as well as adults. It embodies one lesson for us all. Never, ever, let your computer do all your thinking!" **Jo Rogers,** *Myshelf.com*

"Kids will be drawn into this timely sci-fi adventure about a boy who mysteriously becomes a character in his own computer game. The intriguing plot and growing suspense will hold their attention all the way through to the book's provocative ending." **Carol Dengle,** *Dallas Public Library*

"This zoom-paced sci-fi adventure, set in the kingdom of Zaul, is a literary version of every kid's dream of a computer game. *Keeper of the Kingdom* may be touted for youngsters from 9 to 13, but I'll bet you my Spiderman ring that it will be a "sleeper" for adults as well." **Johanna Brewer,** *Plano Star Courier*

Keeper of the Realm

"Ralles' creation may well be a dream come true for some readers. The young adult audience is rife with gamers who should thoroughly enjoy Matt's adventures . . . Watching a young man the age of Matt use his wits to navigate the complicated obstacles and decisions at each level of the game is a good reminder that the young are capable of great things. . . Ralles knows her audience and she gives them what they want. No doubt her fans are already champing at the bit, waiting for *Keeper of the Empire*. It's coming. Practice some of that patience video games reward." **Lisa DuMond SF Site, MEviews.com**

Keeper of the Realm is an exciting sequel to *Keeper of the Kingdom*. This is a great read for young adults, though many young teens will also enjoy it. H.J. Ralles gets better with each book she writes." **Jo Rogers, Myshelf.com**

"This book stands alone as a captivating read for young gamers and sci-fi fans, though the series'intriguing plot line will draw them to want to follow Matt through to the completion of all the levels of his computer game. Evidently Matt will not be returning home as soon as he had wished." **Carol Dengle, Dallas Public Library**

"H.J. Ralles spins a wonderful Science Fiction tale aimed at younger readers, but has also created something that is quite enjoyable for booklovers of all ages. Younger readers will instantly like Matt and his friends and will be eager to learn what is going to happen next. Overall, *Keeper of the Realm* is an excellent read for young readers that enjoy a fantastic yarn and full of surprises that will keep them guessing what will happen next." **Conan Tigard, Book Browser**

"H.J. Ralles continues to offer readers a fascinating affiliation between computers and books. Her two "Keeper" stories are wonderful reading experiences, constructed to keep the pages turning from beginning to end. . . . Players of computer games will see themselves as right in the middle of the game, rather than simply watching on the monitor. **JoAn Martin, Review of Texas Books**

Darok 9

"*Darok 9* is an exciting post-apocalyptic story about the Earth's last survivors, barely enduring on the harsh surface of the moon . . . An enjoyable and recommended novel for science fiction enthusiasts."
The Midwest Book Review

"Ralles holds us to the end in her tension-filled suspense. We read on to see what surprising events her interesting characters initiate. The scientific jargon and technology does not interfere with the action-filled story which any person can follow even if less versed in the science fiction aspects." **JoAn Martin, *Review of Texas Books***

"*Darok 9* has the excitement of a computer game, put into a book, that parents and teachers will love to see in the hands of their children." **Linda Wills, *Rockwall County News***

"*Darok 9* is another wonderful science fiction book for young adults by H.J. Ralles, author of *Keeper of the Kingdom*. Filled with nonstop action and suspense, it tells the story of a young scientist, Hank Havard, and his quest to keep his big discovery out of enemy hands. The Language in this book is clean, as it was in *Keeper of the Kingdom*, something I found refreshing. Also, the message that violence doesn't pay is strong. The characters are believable, and the plot is solid. Darok 9 is a can't-put-it-down, go-away-and-let-me-read science fiction thriller, sure to please any reader of any age!" **Jo Rogers*, Myshelf.com***

"From the first page, the pace of the book is fast and always keeps the reader interested. Young adults will love the suspense that builds and builds as Hank and Will try to avoid being captured." **Conan Tigard, *Book Browser.com***

"*Darok 9* certainly can hold its own in the adult world. This very entertaining book is hard to put down . . . Filled with action and surprises around every bend." **Kelly Hoffman, *Slacker's Sci-Fi Source***

Keeper

of the

Empire

Keeper

of the

Empire

By

H.J. Ralles

Top Publications, Ltd.
Dallas, Texas

KEEPER OF THE EMPIRE

A Top Publications Paperback

Second Edition
12221 Merit Drive, Suite 950
Dallas, Texas 75251

ISBN#: 1-929976-25-9
Library of Congress 2003111465

Printed in the United States of America

For
Megan, Mathew, Robyn and Adam

May you always find pleasure in a good book.

Acknowledgments

Many thanks to: Malcolm, Richard and Edward–as ever, my trusted critics and ardent supporters; Brenda Quinn and Carolyn Williamson, for the many hours of editing which made this book what it is; Bill Manchee and all at Top Publications, who continue to believe in Matt and his adventures; my friends in the Plano Writers, the SCBWI and NAWW whose opinions are invaluable and whose critiquing skills are exceptional; Motophoto, Plano, for great publicity photographs; and my family and friends whose encouragement spurs me on to finish another manauscript.

Chapter 1

Matt rolled onto his back, dazed and disoriented. He squinted to see, blinded by the light from the brilliant sun. *Wonder where I am this time?* he thought.

Tall corn stalks surrounded him. They rustled gently in the breeze, dancing above his head. He sat up slowly and brushed the loose dirt from the sleeves of his denim jacket.

A girl screamed.

Matt tensed.

"Get your dirty great claws off me!" she protested.

"Be still, young lady," a gruff voice replied. "Don't make it worse than it already is."

Matt lay back down. He turned carefully onto his stomach and listened to the commotion.

"I won't cooperate with the likes of a Vorg!" the girl snapped. "You Vorgs are the most hideous things that *ever* walked on two legs."

"All renegades will be caught and desensitized. It is in your best interests to accompany me peacefully."

"Never!"

"So be it," the Vorg growled. "You *will* be desensitized and sent to The Gilded State. It is useless to fight me."

"The Gilded State? Is *that* what you call it? I'd rather

die, you sorry excuse for a life-form!"

Desensitization? What was that? It didn't sound like something Matt wanted to experience. His heart pounded. The brilliant day and idyllic setting seemed to take on a sinister air. He heard the girl shriek. The sounds of scuffling and struggling grew louder as they came through the field, closer and closer to where he hid.

The corn stalks swayed in a gust of wind. Matt dug his fingernails into the earth. If he shifted his position, the unnatural movement of the corn would give him away. He pressed his cheek flat against the ground, willing himself to be still.

Seconds later, right in front of his face, legs thrashed and flailed between the stalks. He held his breath, praying that they would pass by without seeing him. A huge, thick-soled brown boot came to rest inches from his left hand. The urge to run was overwhelming, but Matt lay stone still.

"Okay, just a few more feet to the road. Then I'll get you in the airbug with the others," the Vorg growled.

"Ouch! Let go of my hair, you oaf!"

"Quit complaining, girl. Don't make me use my venom. I really don't want to inflict further pain on you."

"Then set me free, you grotesque being!"

"My, you have spirit to match that mop of curly red hair. Pity. You'll not have such a fiery personality much longer."

"You just wait . . . no Vorg will *ever* break me!" the girl yelled.

"That's what they all say. Desensitization will be over before you can count to ten, and then I *guarantee* you'll be tame."

"Never!"

"Where's your name tag, girl?"

Matt heard the jingling of a metal chain and a deep-bellied laugh.

"Angel? Ha! Your mother got it wrong. Devil would have been more appropriate."

The girl spat.

"Learn some manners!" shouted the Vorg. "I warned you! Now you'll see what my venom can do!"

Matt heard a loud smack followed by a muffled cry. He listened for more of the girl's objections, but she was silent. Only a loud hiss broke the peace of the countryside.

The Vorg turned, and the enormous boot crunched Matt's fingers. His eyes watered with the pain. He counted to ten silently and bit his lip so hard that he tasted blood. *If only they would leave!* Then, as if someone heard his thoughts, the loud rustling of the corn returned to a quiet whisper. Had the Vorg dragged the girl away?

"Hey, Renx. Keep the airbug open," shouted the Vorg. "I've caught another one—she's a real hothead."

The voices faded. Then the high-pitched whirring of an engine and the rushing of air overpowered the sounds of nature, peaceful and reassuring.

Matt's fingertips throbbed. He remained motionless,

listening carefully as the whirring sounds disappeared. A few minutes seemed like forever. After a while his breathing relaxed and he allowed himself to move. He cautiously inched to his knees and then got to his feet, crouching so that he could just see above the ripening husks.

The field of corn stretched as far as he could see, rippling like an ocean under a gentle wind. A long dirt track, only feet from where he hid, wound its way across the expanse of green and out of sight between the distant scrubby oaks.

Matt stood upright. His eyes caught movement in the stalks close by. He ducked in panic.

"Matt . . . hey, Matt, it's me!" came a soft voice.

Matt sighed with relief at the familiar sound of his friend and stood up again. Not far in front of him, a thin, frightened face, framed by straggly blond hair, popped up.

"Targon, you made it here!"

"Looks like I did." Targon sneezed, and rubbed his nose vigorously with the back of his hand. "I think I'm allergic to this stuff." He sneezed again. "I pinched my nose while those goons were dragging off that poor girl."

"I felt really bad for not helping her," said Matt, "but I didn't know what I could do on my own." He swept the husks back with his hands, walking forward to meet Targon halfway. "I didn't dare take a look even though they were so close to me. I was pretty scared. The Vorg stepped on my hand." He held it out.

"It looks bad," said Targon, studying Matt's swollen fingers. "I think you'll just have to suffer a while. There won't be any ice around here."

"That guy must have weighed a ton."

"Guy?"

"Yeah, that's got to be the biggest boot I've ever seen on a human being! His feet were at least ten sizes bigger than mine—and that's saying something."

"Those goons didn't look like any kind of human to me!"

Matt looked up from his red fingers and stared blankly at Targon. "What do you mean? You actually dared to take a look? And you keep saying *goons* as if there was more than one."

Targon nodded and sneezed again. "At least two—if not three . . . and they weren't *men* who took that girl. They were . . . um . . . I don't know what they were—but they definitely weren't human."

"Well, I heard her call him a Vorg—but I assumed he was from a place called Vorg."

"Well, you assumed wrong."

"Were they androids?"

Targon shook his head. "Don't think so."

"Well, what were they? Then at least I'll know when I run into one."

"Oh, you'll know. You won't miss an eight-foot walking reptile with stubby jaws and rolls of skin under his chin . . .oh, and spikes down the back of its neck." He chewed his nails.

Matt chuckled. "Very funny. Good joke. Oh—and they just happen to be bright green, speak English and wear clothes, right?"

Targon looked over his shoulder nervously. Matt waited for him to break into laughter, but Targon turned back and just stared at him with wide eyes.

"You're *not* joking, are you?" said Matt, recognizing his friend's uneasiness.

Targon removed his fingers from his mouth and clenched his fist. "Deadly serious. I've never seen anything like them. Besides, *you* shouldn't be surprised. This is *your* computer game we're in. After meeting the Cybergons in Zaul and then the Noxerans in Karn, what did you expect on the third level?"

Matt shuddered. He suddenly felt like he should hide. He ducked beneath the stalks and yanked on Targon's tunic top until he sat down too. His voice turned to a whisper. "You're right, of course. The game instructions did warn that this level of *Keeper of the Kingdom* would be an even bigger challenge."

"Well, here we are in Level 3. I can't say I'm looking forward to dealing with the Vorgs—they make the Noxerans look like fairies."

Matt smiled briefly. "I think I'm glad I didn't have the guts to look at one." He sighed and looked up at the tops of the waving corn. "You haven't seen Varl, have you?"

"Let's hope he's somewhere close, and we find him before one of those creatures does. Have you got your computer?"

"No," Matt replied. "Once again I've arrived with nothing but the clothes I'm wearing."

"Oh well, we may be lucky and find it," said Targon, starting to retrace his steps.

Matt could feel his friend's despair. He got to his knees and crawled in the dirt until he reached the area where the corn had been flattened by his arrival. Matt peered through the stalks in all directions. Where was his computer? Searching for a needle in a haystack was an appropriate cliché to describe his situation, he decided. His computer could be anywhere in this enormous field. Even if he took days to search it thoroughly, he probably wouldn't find it. Discouraged, he crawled back to Targon, trying not to put pressure on his throbbing fingers.

"Impossible, if you ask me," Matt said, sitting cross-legged. He sighed deeply.

Targon nudged him in the ribs. "This happen to be yours?" He produced a black laptop computer with a cracked case from behind his back.

Matt grinned and took it from his friend. "Great going, Targon! We're in luck this time!"

Targon beamed. "Well, come on. Don't waste any more time. Open it up before those Vorgs return, and tell me what we've got to do to win Level 3 of your *Keeper of the Kingdom* game. I thought you wanted to get home!"

"Of course I do!" said Matt, eagerly raising the lid.

The sky suddenly darkened and a shadow fell across the corn. The birds stopped singing. A deafening drumming broke the peacefulness of the countryside. Matt covered his ears and looked up. Targon did the same. An enormous elliptical object came rushing down toward them. Matt threw his arms over his head, thinking that he was about to be crushed to death. He held his breath and waited. But nothing happened.

When he realized that he was still alive, Matt dared to lift his head. The object hovered above them, filling the sky. Matt's head ached with the constant pulsating noise. Should they make a run for it?

The object came lower. Matt gulped. His heart raced. Targon grabbed his sleeve.

Then, as quickly as the object had descended, it zoomed off into the distance. The sunlight returned, the drumming noise subsided, and the birds began to sing again.

Matt drew in a deep breath.

"What . . . what was that?" Targon stammered.

"If I had to make a guess, I'd say it was a UFO."

"A what?"

"An unidentified flying object—you know, a flying saucer," repeated Matt.

"What's a flying saucer?" Targon whispered. "I've never seen one before."

"Neither have I," said Matt. "But that sure looked like descriptions I've heard." He scrambled to his feet, and with shaking knees dared to peer over the corn husks. The elliptical object was still visible, hovering on the horizon. Matt watched with keen interest. He didn't believe in UFOs, but he could find no other explanation for this strange thing. Finally it disappeared from sight.

Matt sat down again and looked at his friend's blank expression.

"So, what *is* a flying saucer?" Targon asked again.

"It's a spaceship that comes from another planet."

"Oh," said Targon, who looked stunned by the explanation.

"Yeah, exactly," said Matt, hardly believing what he had just seen.

"Do you think they'll be back for us?"

Matt sighed. "I hope not. We don't know if they saw us or if they were looking for humans like the Vorgs who took that girl away." He swallowed hard as an awful thought dawned upon him. "Say, Targon, I hope we're still on Earth. You don't think this is another planet, do you?"

Targon shrugged. "What did your game rules say?"

Matt picked up his computer. He ran his good hand over the lid as he thought back to the time when he ripped open the *Keeper of the Kingdom* box and read the game instructions. "The instructions said something like 'Save the people and defeat the Keeper on Earth in 2540 AD.'"

"So, wouldn't they have mentioned another planet?"

Matt stared at the closed laptop. "I guess so. In Level 1 of my game, Zaul was a kingdom on *Earth* in 2540 and in Level 2, Karn was an underwater realm on *Earth* in 2540. I must admit, this *feels* like Earth. In fact, this place looks very much like the area around my hometown."

Targon got to his feet. "Well, wherever we are, I don't much feel like sitting in a cornfield all night. Vorgs could return at any minute, and there's nowhere to hide. Try to run in this field and they'd catch us easily."

"I agree," said Matt. "It's not safe here. We ought to find somewhere better. When we do, I'll open my game instructions, and perhaps we'll have some clue as to where we are."

"So, which way do we go?"

"Let's stay low in the corn until we reach the edge of the field and then follow the track past those oaks. We can't see much else from here."

Targon shuddered. "It would be nice if this *were* your hometown."

"Somehow I don't think we'll be so lucky. There aren't any Vorgs where I come from!"

* * * * *

"Let's rest a while," suggested Targon, as the dirt track ended and they reached a main road. "We've been walking for ages."

"Sure," said Matt, leaning against a tree trunk at the edge of the road. He placed his computer at his feet, squatted down and looked at his watch. "We've been going for nearly three hours, so we've probably walked about nine or ten miles."

"How's your hand?" asked Targon, sitting on a rotting tree stump.

Matt wiggled his fingers. "Getting better, thanks. I'll survive. It'll just be sore for a few days. Don't think I broke any bones."

"Any idea which way we should go?"

The land was flat for as far as Matt could see in any direction, but dotted with trees and scraggy bushes. Down the road to his left, he could just make out a white house and a distant bank of trees merging with the early evening sky. He examined the road in that direction. It was in a terrible state of disrepair. The concrete surface was severely broken with huge cracks. It would be difficult to walk on in the dark.

Lights began to flicker in the distance. Man-made illumination was replacing the gentle radiance from the setting sun. "See the yellow glow?" he said to Targon. "Well, if this *is* my home in the U.S.A., that would be the glow of city lights."

"So you think we should go left?"

Matt yawned. "Heading toward the lights seems like our best bet. We might find somewhere comfortable to spend the night." He picked up his laptop.

"Okay, let's go then," said Targon. "I'm all for finding somewhere to sleep."

Targon hopped over the crevices in the road as if he were playing a game. Within minutes he was several yards in front.

"Don't know how you can see to go so fast," shouted

Matt, stumbling over the uneven surface. "I'm virtually blind in this dim light."

Targon stopped and turned to his right. "Another field, and another field, *and* another field" he moaned. "Apart from the rare barn that we've passed, the landscape is *so* boring around here."

"But the open spaces feel great," replied Matt, catching up. He sighed and added, "Just like at home."

Matt ached as he remembered all the lazy summer afternoons down by the brook, exploring the countryside with his friends. Lying in the cornfield earlier that afternoon, the surroundings had felt so familiar—the tall ripening corn in the warm breeze, the brilliant sun, the unforgettable deep blue sky and even the humid smell.

"This *could* be home," Matt thought out loud.

"Look, I know you want to go home badly, but I think you'd better drop the idea that this is it. You said this afternoon that you didn't have Vorgs where you come from."

Matt could just make out Targon's honest expression in the near darkness. His friend was right, of course, but it was hard to accept the truth.

"I'm sorry," Targon said softly. "It's great if you *are* home, but . . ."

"It's okay—you're right," mumbled Matt. "It was just my wishful thinking."

Targon gasped. "Get down—there's something parked in the field!"

Matt ducked and scrambled on all fours next to his

friend at the road's edge. His heart beat a little faster.

"Where?" he whispered, peering over a ditch full of water and into the grassy field beyond.

"Over there. Do you see it?"

Matt could only just make out the outline of a dome shape in the darkening sky. Suddenly, a high-pitched whirring of an engine—the same sound that he had heard in the cornfield—broke the silence of the sleeping countryside. Powerful lights illuminated the field. The object rose a few feet off the ground and hovered while searchlights rhythmically swept across the grass.

Targon moved closer and clenched Matt's arm. Matt could feel his friend shaking.

"It's another airbug," whispered Targon.

Matt gulped. "And that means more Vorgs."

Chapter 2

The smell of burning rubber was repulsive. Varl lifted his arm and used the wide sleeve of his robe to cover his nose. He turned in circles, scanning the room, hoping to find Matt or Targon. They were nowhere to be seen and he had no idea where he was. He could not see any chemicals, medicines, or foods that could cause such a stench on any of the long countertops. Varl thought he was in some kind of laboratory, but four black cushioned beds on pedestals and the lack of science equipment suggested otherwise. *Am I in a doctor's clinic?* he wondered.

The sudden sound of a shrill bell caught his attention. Varl focused on a huge cylindrical chamber in the center of the room. Two yellow lights flashed alternately above the clear container. An electrical current sparked and flickered through the glass. Then a magnificent display of metallic green shapes swirled up and down inside.

As Varl stood mesmerized by the brilliance of the chamber, images appeared to be forming within. Immediately he recognized the early signs of a materialization in progress. Within seconds, life-forms would appear. He had no idea whether the inhabitants of this place were hostile or friendly, and he wasn't about to stay and find out.

Varl scanned the room for somewhere to hide. There were no closets or cupboards. His gaze fell on an examination table in the far corner. On one side was a floor-to-ceiling curtain hanging from a track, which could be drawn around the table to separate the corner from the rest of the room.

Varl crept past the sparking chamber and tugged at the curtain. It slid smoothly along the metal rail. He pulled it past the examination table, enclosing it.

"Come on old man, you can do it," he muttered, eyeing the low shelf across the bottom of the table. He groaned as he lowered himself to the floor. With great effort, he slithered on his belly and forced his way underneath the shelf. The cold floor tiles chilled his bones through his thin white robe.

Another bell sounded. Voices carried across the room. Varl guessed that the materialization had finished and the chamber had opened. He lifted the bottom edge of the curtain. All he could see were a dozen pairs of bare human feet.

"Line them up against the wall."

The depth and huskiness of the voice perplexed Varl. He lifted the curtain higher and strained his neck for a better look. A pair of enormous brown boots moved directly in front of his eyes.

Two fat, scaly, green ankles extended up from the boots. He gasped and jerked his head upward, hitting his head hard on the shelf.

"Ouch!" Varl exclaimed, his head throbbing. Instantly he realized his mistake. The curtain was whipped back and a strong pair of arms dragged him out from underneath the table. Claw-like hands dug into his calves.

"Get up, old man!" ordered a voice.

Using his hands to push himself off the floor, Varl struggled slowly to his feet. As he rose, his eyes traveled up the pair of hefty legs clothed in tight brown, leathery pants. Finally upright, he looked directly at a massive mottled-green chest, which protruded from an open yellow vest. Varl rarely felt *real* fear. But on this occasion, he trembled as he tipped his head to gaze upon his captor's face towering above him.

Atop a thick scaly neck sat the distorted head of a reptile that Varl would have normally expected to see in a zoo. The talking creature resembled a large iguana. Black slits in its beady yellow eyes seemed to focus on him. Conical white spikes protruded from the back of the creature's head. Varl could only stare. Was he dreaming? He staggered backwards. The words *Amblyrhynchus cristatus, the Marine Iguana,* popped into his head. Varl racked his brains trying to remember everything he had read about such a reptile. One thing was certain—no iguana he had ever read about walked on two feet or spoke English!

"Line up with the others!" the reptile ordered.

In his shock, Varl hardly noticed the line of subdued humans standing with their backs to the wall. He shuffled next to a thin woman, his eyes never leaving the reptilian face.

"I am Jesper of the Mount, a Vorg Commander," the creature said in guttural tones. "You are about to be sent to The Gilded State. You will not be disappointed with the results. Desensitization is painless and takes only minutes. It will remove your worries and bring you much happiness."

The Vorg's words snapped Varl back to reality. He looked down the line of men and women, wondering why they were here. The woman standing next to him rocked back and forth. Another chewed her nails. Most stared straight ahead, their expressions fixed. They seemed accepting of their fate, but Varl felt sure he could see fear in their eyes. What was The Gilded State? What was desensitization? Who was this Jesper of the Mount?

Four other Vorgs stood next to each of the padded examination beds. He doubted that he could overpower the massive creatures on his own. Varl wondered what choice he had, if any, but to accept The Gilded State.

Jesper of the Mount tapped four men on their shoulders. "First four," he said in a calm manner.

One man refused to move. Jesper snarled. His long red tongue lashed out close to the man's face.

"Do you want a dose of my venom?" he growled.

The man shook his head and without further objection joined the other three. They walked to the beds and lay down. The Vorgs placed a helmet fitted with a plastic visor over the head of each man. A cable ran from each helmet to a central console.

"Adjust beds," instructed Jesper, walking to the console.

A sound like a jackhammer filled the room. The beds rose several feet on the pedestals until each of the helmet cables was taut.

"Begin desensitization."

Varl waited. The room was quiet. No sound or visible sign indicated that the process had begun. He looked in turn at each of the men lying on beds. There was no movement, no evidence of pain, and no recognition on their faces that anything bad was happening.

Jesper of the Mount seemed to smile. Inside his open mouth Varl saw the long lumpy tongue rolled up tightly and tiny sharp teeth. He shuddered at the thought of making this creature angry.

Time ticked slowly by. The vile rubbery smell that Varl had almost become accustomed to was now overpowering. Several minutes later, the beds were lowered to their original position. The Vorgs removed the helmets, and each man rose from his bed. With fixed wide grins they turned to Jesper and in unison announced: "We are thankful for The Gilded State."

Varl watched with horror. The little bit of personality that he had seen in each man before the desensitization process had disappeared. Behind each pair of human eyes there seemed to be no recognition, no appreciation of who they were or where they were, and no feelings of any kind. It was as if their spirit had been sucked out of them. Four zombies, not four humans, headed for the open materialization chamber.

Varl watched them step inside. The bell rang, and the transparent door slid back into place. Lights flashed, sparks flew and the four desensitized humans were dematerialized before his eyes. The glass chamber was empty. In a few minutes Varl knew he would have to accept the same fate.

The next four humans were sent to the beds. Varl felt the heat rise from his fingertips up to his neck as panic set in. His breaths were short and raspy. He was too old to take on even one Vorg. The helmets were on, and the beds had risen. He had to escape. His eyes scanned the room for something he could use as a weapon. There was nothing. The stark room had few furnishings and no equipment. Time was running out.

The procedure finished a second time. Varl watched the newly desensitized people thank Jesper of the Mount for The Gilded State and walk stoically toward the chamber. He looked from the open door to the beds. He made his choice. He was not about to be sent to The Gilded State.

The bell sounded. As the last of the four humans stepped into the materialization chamber, Varl broke from the line and raced toward the closing door. He leaped through the narrow gap, yanking the end of his robe from the crack as the door slid shut.

Varl saw Jesper of the Mount's penetrating yellow

eyes stare at him. His jaws were wide open, and his long tongue lashed against the glass in anger. The few seconds that it had taken the creature to realize what was happening had saved Varl.

"Stop   him!"   Jesper   bellowed.   "Stop   the dematerialization process!"

"It's too late! Dematerialization has begun!" replied one of the Vorgs who had rushed to the console. "There's nothing we can do."

Varl   barely   heard   the   reply.   He   watched apprehensively as his fingers and feet disappeared. Only then did he think about dematerialization. Where was he headed? Would he ever be whole again?

Chapter 3

M att lay perfectly still in the cool night air, his heart pounding against his chest. He could hear Targon's heavy breathing next to him. The full moon created an eerie atmosphere. Its silvery light glimmered through the trees, casting haunting shadows on the ground. The fields that had felt so familiar to Matt that afternoon now felt hostile. Matt had tucked the laptop inside his denim jacket, as he had done before. The corners dug into his ribs. He winced and tried to alter his position without making any noticeable movement.

The airbug crept toward them, sweeping every inch of the field with its searchlights.

"Do you think they saw us?" Targon whispered.

"Could be," replied Matt. "Don't move. Maybe we'll get lucky."

The huge dome hovered close to the ditch. The air from under its wide rubber skirt blew the grass flat in every direction. Flying stones and dust stung Matt's face. The piercing white lights blinded him. He tried to remain calm, but it was difficult. The thought of facing a Vorg caused the blood to race through his veins.

"Humans, remain still where we can see you," boomed a voice from the airbug. "If you do not comply, you will suffer the consequences."

"What do we do?" yelled Targon, barely audible above the noise of rushing air.

"We run!" shouted Matt. "I'm not letting them have my computer, and I sure don't want to be desensitized!"

"Okay, I'm with you. Where to?"

"We passed a barn back there. We might make it," Matt replied, already off the ground and running. "Come on, Targon!"

He focused on the crumbling building lit up by the airbug's powerful lights, and didn't look back. The uneven road made it impossible to run fast. Matt stumbled and lurched as he tried to keep his balance while clutching a laptop to his chest. Targon was on his heels, puffing and panting.

"Just a few more yards," shouted Matt, without looking behind.

"And then what?" Targon yelled.

Matt didn't take the time to answer. He doubted they could outrun an airbug, and he had no idea how they could defend themselves against an enemy such as Targon had described. His mind raced. One thing was clear: he had to hide his computer.

Matt reached the barn first. He pulled at the huge crumbling wooden doors, one at a time, with his good hand. Neither budged. Bits of rotten wood fell to the ground. He clutched the computer through his jacket while struggling to get his breath.

Targon arrived, gasping. "It's useless. The airbug's already landed on the road. They'll be here any minute."

"The barn doors won't move. The wood's too rotten. I've got to get rid of my computer. Help me think of something! Quick!"

"Over there . . . by the door—is that a water trough?" asked Targon, hardly able to spit out the words.

Matt looked to the right of the doors. A rusty old animal trough, mounted on a thick concrete base, sat close to the barn. In the low light he could just make out a narrow space between the trough and the barn wall.

"The Vorgs are coming!" whispered Targon, moving in front of Matt to block him. "Hide it now!"

Matt opened his jacket, pulled out the laptop and forced it down into the gap. He turned around just as two Vorgs, illuminated by the airbug's lights, leaped across the ditch and headed toward them. They carried powerful flashlights.

"Good hiding place, Targon," he muttered, stepping away from the barn. "If we get separated and you find Varl, remember where it is."

"And where *is* this, exactly?" asked Targon. He raised his eyebrows and contorted his face into a twisted grin.

"*Some* barn in the middle of . . . *some*where," replied Matt, his heart sinking when he realized how futile hiding his laptop had been.

"Exactly," whispered Targon. "And this place won't look the same in daylight, either. We'll never find it again."

Matt inched closer to Targon as the two huge

creatures approached. Blinded by their flashlights, he strained to see their features. Then suddenly, one Vorg was illuminated by the beam of the other's flashlight. Matt gasped. Even with Targon's description, he still couldn't believe what he saw. The strange mix of reptilian features and the spiked head were straight out of a prehistoric tale.

One Vorg scowled. Matt watched his forehead crease into thick ripples of leathery skin, which hung like huge eyebrows over his mesmerizing yellow eyes.

He turned to the other and snorted. "Renx, I told you that humans are slow learners."

"You didn't seriously think you could outrun our airbug, did you?" Renx laughed with a deep hiss. He stood with his arms folded across his broad chest and legs spread apart. "But Urg and I enjoyed watching you try, nevertheless."

Matt took a step backward. In Renx's voice he recognized the huskiness he'd heard earlier in the cornfield. Angel's words replayed in his mind. The girl had put up a good fight. He knew he had to divert their attention away from the barn and his computer.

"We . . .we're . . . we're not coming peacefully," Matt stammered.

Targon shot him a horrorstruck glance. "We're not?" he questioned.

Matt glared at him.

"I mean—no, we're not," said Targon, changing his tone.

"Oh, you're not?" Urg laughed. "And just where do you think you *are* going?"

"Anywhere but with Vorgs!" Matt retorted, finding the courage to spit out the words.

Renx's wide toothy grin disappeared, and he frowned, folds of skin gathering at the top of his snout.

"Look, boy. You know the rules," reasoned Renx. "Save yourself a lot of pain. Choose to come peacefully, and you'll be rewarded with a trip to The Gilded State. Cause us trouble, and you'll regret it. A Vorg's venom is not pleasant."

Matt took several more steps backward. Targon copied him.

"What *is* it with humans today?" Urg threw his fat, stubby arms open in puzzlement. "They *never* learn!"

Matt turned to run. He had only taken two steps when he felt something strong whip around his waist, pull tight and reel him in. He looked down to see what had ensnared him. Urg's long red tongue was wrapped around his middle.

Renx laughed loudly, hissing between his teeth with each breath. "You can't outrun an airbug and you can't outrun a Vorg."

"Let go of me, you . . . you . . .." Matt growled, struggling to loosen the thick tongue crushing his ribs. His hands felt suddenly warm and wet. A sticky green slime oozed between his fingers.

"Ugh!" He heaved, repulsed by the putrid smell. Then his body went numb. He couldn't move. His brain was still alert. He heard everything, but he could say and do nothing.

"The young man's just learned his lesson," said Renx, laughing. His jovial manner disappeared and his face took on a menacing grin. "A Vorg's venom is to be feared." He turned to look at Targon and snarled. "The other one won't cause us any trouble now—will you?"

The long tongue sprang back inside Urg's mouth as quickly as it had shot out. The Vorg's claws stabbed into Matt's arm, holding him upright in a vice-like grip.

Targon shook his head and stammered, "N-n-no t-t-trouble."

Matt could see his friend's pale face and shaking knees, but he couldn't open his mouth to reassure Targon that he was not in any pain.

Urg dragged Matt to the waiting airbug. He couldn't feel the ground bumping under his feet. Targon walked silently alongside.

A narrow door slid upward and into the roof of the vehicle. Targon was shoved inside. Renx roughly pushed Matt onto the floor. He lay looking at the ceiling. A white light shone down into his face. Matt was still unable to move a limb or utter a word. He couldn't even blink to shield his eyes from the brightness of the bulb. The door slammed shut.

"Zang it! Are you okay?" asked Targon. He bent over Matt and stared into his eyes.

But all Matt could do was stare back at his friend.

* * * * *

Varl watched his legs and hands materialize. The strange sensation began with a tingling in his fingertips and ended with a feeling that someone was sticking thousands of pins into every nerve of his body. He wiggled his fingers. All his body parts were accounted for and back in the right place. When the curved door of the materialization chamber opened, he stepped onto the sidewalk. He was standing on a street corner amidst the tall elegant structures of a busy city.

Varl's mouth dropped in astonishment as he surveyed his new neighborhood. He looked up and down the street, hardly believing what he was seeing. The city was every architect's dream with its unusual shaped buildings and graceful sculptures. Not a trace of trash was visible anywhere. So clean were the streets that Varl felt he would be able to eat a meal off the pristine sidewalk.

Skyscrapers towered overhead on both sides of the road. The sun reflected off thousands of panes of glass, which were angled in every direction. Domed vehicles lifted into the air as if by magic. With a faint whirring noise and a rush of air, they sped past, navigating around other traffic.

Varl's attention turned to the few individuals who walked along the sidewalks. They were all clothed in green baggy pants, long-sleeved tops and white tennis shoes. Varl could not see even one person dressed in anything different. Males and females looked alike. Even their hairstyles were eerily similar. Their short, neat cuts with heavy bangs made Varl think that he was looking at a collection of living dolls. Their permanent smiles made Varl wonder if these people were walking in heaven.

"The Gilded State, huh!" Varl muttered. "Is this what humans are turned into?"

Varl ducked into an entrance to one of the skyscrapers. He had to find somewhere to hide. The Vorgs wouldn't waste any time sending out a search party. Varl gazed down at his white robe and leather moccasins. He looked out of place. To avoid capture, he would have to blend into this strange environment.

I've got to get rid of this robe and find a disguise, he thought. *But how?*

Varl peered around the corner of the covered entrance. There were no Vorgs in sight. Acting like a zombie, he walked with his head high and a fixed smile on his face to the entrance of the next building. Two marble columns framed a tiled porch. An old man leaned back against the wooden doors, staring into the street. He looked through Varl as if he weren't there.

Varl took a deep breath. "Where is this place?" he dared to ask.

"Don't you just love The Gilded State?" the old man replied.

"Yes, really," said Varl, astounded by the question. He studied the blank face and vacant eyes of a man at least twenty years older than himself. It was as if the man had lost his mind. Varl's chest tightened, but he knew there was nothing he could do to help him. He looked at the old man's green outfit. It was exactly the disguise he needed to blend in. Dare he ask the man to trade clothes? He decided that he had to take the risk. Vorgs could materialize at any minute.

"How would you like to exchange your clothes for my robe—just for a time?"

"Don't you just love The Gilded State?" asked the old man again. He looked briefly at Varl with expressionless gray eyes.

Varl sighed. He began removing his robe, half-expecting questions, but the man asked none. Still grinning, he handed Varl his top, and then his pants and tennis shoes.

"Don't you just love The Gilded State?" the man repeated as he slipped Varl's long robe over his perfect hair.

Varl grunted his reply. "It's a great place for a vacation."

He hurriedly dressed in the drab clothes. The pants were a little short and the top tight across his shoulders, but they were adequate. He looked down at his feet. He'd had his comfy brown moccasins for years. They would have to go. If he were going to blend in, he had to do it properly. Varl's heart wrenched as he pulled the moccasins off and slipped them over the man's frail feet.

Varl crammed his toes into the tennis shoes,

straightened himself, and drew in a deep breath. He really had no idea what to do next, or where to go.

"Psst!"

"Who's there?" Varl asked. He swung around to see a youthful tanned face peering round the column.

"Come 'ere," said the young teen, beckoning to Varl. His ebony eyes were wide and inviting.

"Pardon?"

"Come 'ere!" he said with gusto.

Varl hesitated. His pulse quickened. *Was this a trap?* The boy's clothes and accent were different from the old man's. Why hadn't the boy been sent to The Gilded State like everyone else?

"It's now or never, mate. Are you comin' with me or not?"

The boy disappeared behind the column. Varl's curiosity got the better of him. What did he have to lose by following? If he stayed where he was, the Vorgs would find him. Varl chased after the tall wiry teenager, wincing in pain occasionally as his knees gave way. He was becoming arthritic in his old age, and escapades like this pushed him to the limits.

The boy wove in and out of entrances, hid behind parked airbugs, and paused before running past the materialization chambers on every corner. Varl focused on the lanky figure for fear of losing him. All the time the boy seemed alert, checking in every direction before venturing on. Never did he look behind to see if Varl were following.

Varl found the fast pace tiring. He caught up, panting heavily, only to watch the boy's long legs dart across another road.

They reached an elaborate building with two revolving doors. Varl followed the boy into the foyer.

"What is this place?" Varl asked, finally catching up to him.

The boy smiled, displaying crooked front teeth, and quickly looked around the foyer. "No time to talk now. It's all clear, so are you comin', mate?"

The boy ran to a staircase in the corner and disappeared down the stairs. Varl groaned, gripped his pounding chest and ran after him. Hesitating for a second at the top, Varl took hold of the handrail and walked quickly down the narrow steps.

The stairs ended in a cellar. The air was damp and heavy. A solitary light bulb illuminated the crumbling walls. Overhead, black pipes and wires wove in and out of the beams. Varl tried to see in the low light, unsure of which way to turn.

"Psst! Over 'ere."

Varl stared ahead. He could just make out the boy in his black sweatshirt and frayed jeans disappearing round a corner to the right.

"Not again," Varl moaned, exasperated. Was the boy taking him for a fool? He slowed and remained close to the wall. Would he be faced with a row of Vorgs when he turned the corner? There was nothing he could do. If this were a trap, he had walked right into it.

Varl reached the corner. He hesitated and then peered around the edge. The boy was squatting down by a metal circle in the floor. There were no Vorgs in sight.

"I won't go any farther with you until I get some answers," said Varl, standing with his arms folded across his chest.

The boy didn't look up. He pulled at the metal cover. "Give me an 'and, mate. This thing's 'eavy!"

Varl found himself rushing to help the boy. They slid the cover back, exposing an open shaft, that plummeted into darkness. The boy removed his shoes, tied the laces together, and hung them around his neck. Carefully, he lowered himself over the edge and began the descent down a metal ladder.

"Who are you, and where are you taking me?" Varl demanded.

"If you wanna 'ang around and wait for them Vorgs, you can, but I ain't! I suggest you get your shoes off and get down 'ere with me, quick! Oh, and pull the cover back," he shouted up.

Varl looked around the cellar and thought about the danger lurking above. This boy was full of life and thinking rationally—not some zombie of The Gilded State. Perhaps if he followed him, he would get some answers.

Varl removed his tennis shoes and clambered down the ladder, wincing with pain as he stepped on the narrow rungs with bare feet. When only his head was above the floor level, he tugged at the metal cover and heaved it back into place. Now he had closed off the only light. He descended in darkness. He could hear nothing but the sound of trickling water far below. Varl lowered himself rung by rung. He had no idea how far he would fall if he lost his footing. As he brushed his upper body against the ladder, the dangling pair of shoes slipped off his shoulder and fell. Varl listened and listened. Several seconds later he heard a splash.

"You okay, mate?"

Varl smiled to himself in the darkness. The boy's voice echoing up the shaft was a welcome sound. "Yes, I'm fine, thanks. Just lost my shoes."

"Keep comin'. You've got a ways to go."

"Thanks," muttered Varl.

He didn't *really* want to know how far down the shaft went. Step by step he felt for the next rung with his feet and slid his hands down the sides of the ladder. The deeper he went, the colder it became. The ladder felt slippery and wet. Varl shivered. Without sight, his other senses became more acute. A pungent smell suddenly hit his nostrils. Varl gasped and choked. The smell was unmistakable—sewers!

It was a shock when his left foot found water, even though he knew it was coming. Still there was no light. He lowered his right foot alongside the left. Immediately he felt the bottoms of his pants soaking up the filthy water. It was at least six inches deep and he wondered what else he would be treading in.

"Have I reached the bottom?" Varl asked, still gripping the ladder. It seemed a silly question in the circumstances, but he was afraid to let go and walk into the unknown. The boy tugged at his arm.

"You're okay, mate. Just 'ang on to me. I'll take you where you need to go."

"And where's that, exactly?" Varl pinched his nose with one hand and felt for the boy's arm with the other. They began wading.

"Somewhere safe. Away from them Vorgs."

The boy's words were reassuring. Varl relaxed slightly. They walked in silence for a few minutes. The only sound was that of the water sloshing around their ankles and its echo down the pipes.

"What's your name?" Varl asked, not expecting an answer.

"Snake. The name's Snake."

"Pleased to make your acquaintance." Varl coughed again. He felt the need to clear his lungs, but every time he took in a breath, the smell seemed to tighten his chest more.

"And what's *your* name?" Snake asked. The pungent smell didn't seem to have suppressed the boy's lighthearted manner.

"Varl."

"That's a strange one."

"So is Snake," replied Varl.

"Yeah, I s'ppose."

"So, how did you get it?"

"'Cuz no one can slither 'round these sewers like me!" His laughter echoed down the narrow drain.

Varl also laughed, but his laughter turned into a hacking cough. The water became deeper. Varl's pants clung to his knees. His whole body felt chilled.

"You'll be okay in a minute," said Snake as they turned a corner. "You're gonna get fresh air soon . . . I promise."

A faint band of sunlight lit the surface of the water. Varl's eyes began to adjust. For the first time he could see the outline of the huge drain and the water around their knees.

"Time to go up," said Snake, pausing at the bottom of another shaft. "It's a long way. I 'ope you're up to it. Wanna go first?"

Varl cleared his throat and began to climb. "The sooner I get out of here the better."

Scaling the ladder was easy at first. He got into a rhythm of reaching up to the next rung and then heaving himself up another foot.

"You're doin' fine," Snake would say, urging him on whenever he rested for too long.

The climb seemed endless and the daylight never seemed to get any closer. Varl began to pant and gasp. His arms ached. The balls of his feet were sore from pushing on the narrow metal rungs. His arthritic joints grew more painful with every step. It was strenuous exercise for even a young person. He grimaced. Until today he had thought himself fit for a sixty-one-year-old man.

"I've got to rest," Varl announced, finally giving in to

his body.

"Keep goin'. We're almost there," ordered Snake.

Varl linked his right elbow around the next rung, and gripped it with his right hand. Grunting and groaning, he began to pull himself up again.

One foot slipped, then the other. Both feet dangled above Snake. Varl's body flailed sideways. His right arm around the rung was all that prevented him from falling. His long, bony fingers tightened around the bar.

"Ahh!" he yelled in agony. He felt as though his arm had been wrenched from its socket.

"Grab the rung! Grab the rung with your other 'and!" screamed Snake.

Varl lunged for the bar with his left hand. His right hand started to slip.

"Grab it, mate. Do it! If you fall you'll take me too!"

Varl hollered as he lunged for the bar a second time. This time his fingertips curled over the rung. He clung with all his might, Snake's words ringing in his ears. He could not take the life of a young boy.

"Now your feet!" screamed Snake. "Pull 'round. Get that left foot on a bar!"

Varl focused on the ladder. He kicked his legs until he felt one of the rungs against his shins.

"Ahh!" he hollered again.

"Go on, mate," urged Snake.

Varl clenched his teeth, determined to succeed. He heaved his body up and fought to locate the rung.

"Zang it!" Varl muttered as he finally managed to get

both feet on a bar. His heart pounded against his rib cage. He pressed his body up against the ladder and breathed deeply in an effort to regain his composure and slow his heart rate.

After a few minutes of silence Snake said, "How you doin' now, mate?"

Varl detected a tremor in his voice. The boy sounded shaken.

"Fine, I'm fine," Varl replied, trying to sound composed. He knew that somehow he had to find the strength to make it to the top. If he lost his grip again, they might both plummet to their deaths.

Chapter 4

Matt's stomach lurched as the airbug began its descent. He felt as though he were in an elevator that was plunging to the ground. He hated elevators, always scared that they wouldn't stop at the bottom of the shaft.

The airbug's engines slowed. The sound of rushing air was reassuring. The floor vibrated beneath him. It was a good sign. Perhaps he would soon be able to move again.

"I think we're landing," said Targon, his voice quaking.

Matt felt the muscles around his mouth relax. He managed a thin smile, but still couldn't speak.

Targon knelt on the floor and patted him on the shoulder. "You'll be okay," he reassured. "It looks like the venom's wearing off." He pursed his lips and frowned. "It feels like we're hovering. I think they would have turned off the power if we were on the ground."

Matt hated waiting for the unknown. Where had they been taken?

The noise made by the airbug changed. Targon toppled sideways. The engines cut, and there was a loud thud. It was the unmistakable sound of the craft coming to rest.

Seconds later Matt heard the rear door of the airbug

open.

"Out! Now!" hissed one of the Vorgs, shoving Targon.

"Bye, Matt," said Targon quietly. "Hope you're okay. I guess I've got to go where they tell me."

Matt heard him jumping to the ground.

"Now it's your turn, strong-willed human." Matt recognized the huskiness of Renx's voice. "You're a lucky one. You'll be yourself again in a few hours. A Vorg's venom can kill. I gave you a small dose this time. You'd better make sure there isn't a next time!"

Matt was lifted into the air. The blood rushed to his head as he was tossed upside down. It was a bumpy ride on Renx's shoulder, and he could only follow the concrete floor with his eyes as they walked along. He sniffed. There was a distinct rubbery smell. Matt managed to turn his head sideways. Large metal struts lined the walls. He presumed they supported the ceiling, although he couldn't lift his head to see. Every ten steps or so, they passed a shiny silver canister clipped into a bracket on the wall. He wondered what they were.

Renx walked into a clear cylindrical chamber. Matt felt dizzy as Renx lowered him to the floor inside a marked circle.

"This is a materialization chamber," Renx hissed. "The procedure is painless." He stepped out.

Matt watched the clear door slide shut, enclosing him. He looked at Renx through the glass. The Vorg pressed digits on a small computer mounted on the wall beside the chamber. Before Matt had time to think about dematerialization, a tingling sensation raced up his arms. He felt as though he were being pricked by millions of little needles. At first he was pleased because he realized the venom was wearing off rapidly, and he could feel his hands and legs again. Then he watched in horror as his fingers, and then his hands, disappeared.

* * * * *

"Who are you?" asked a female voice.

Matt looked up to see a mop of curly red hair hanging above him. He moved his stiff jaw from side to side with his left hand and slowly sat up in the materialization chamber. His arms and legs shook for a few seconds. He looked through the open door into the tiny room beyond. The walls were red brick, and a narrow rectangular window, up high, let in light.

"I can see the Vorgs gave you a dose of their venom," the girl said, helping Matt to his feet. "You'll feel fine in a little while." She led him through the open door of the chamber.

"You're Angel, aren't you?" said Matt, finding his voice again. The girl looked shocked. She shoved her hands into the back pockets of her tight pants and glared at him. "Who wants to know?"

Matt staggered over to a metal bench in the far corner of the room and sat down. First he massaged his knees and then his elbows. Finally he looked into her striking green eyes and answered. "My name's Matt . . .

Matt Hammond. I was hiding with my friend in the cornfield when one of the Vorgs caught you. I recognize your voice, *and* I heard the Vorg say you had red hair."

She seemed to relax a little and smiled weakly. "Where are you from?"

Matt hesitated, unsure of how to answer. He had no idea where he was or what time period he had landed in. If he told Angel that she was a character in his computer game she'd think he was mad, and if he answered that he was from the U.S.A. in 2010, that could also land him in a heap of trouble. "Here and there," he replied as casually as he could.

"What kind of answer is that?" Angel snapped. She placed her hands on her hips and scowled at him.

Matt felt flustered. This was not going to be easy. "What I mean is . . . that I wander from place to place." *Not altogether untrue*, Matt thought. He decided to divert attention from himself and question her. "Where are you from?"

"Here," she replied, still looking at him with a distrustful expression.

"Where's here?" Matt asked, and then realized his mistake.

Angel looked at him with a twisted grin. She tipped her head to one side, fiddled with one of her dangling gold earrings and said, "Are you for real?"

Matt's face burned with embarrassment. His palms became clammy. He thought quickly. "Sorry, I'm still dazed from the effects of the Vorg's venom. I mean, which side of the town are you from?"

"Town?" she questioned. "This has been Bay City in the Govan Empire for as long as I can remember!"

Matt grinned and added quickly, "My neighborhood had a small-town feel until the Vorgs arrived." He suddenly realized that his last comment could also be wrong. He didn't know how long the Vorgs had been here, or if indeed they had come from somewhere else. He had made those assumptions from Angel's brief conversation with Renx in the cornfield. His heart raced. He waited for her reaction.

She rolled her eyes, stared at him for a minute and finally sat next to him on the bench. "I know what you mean. This was *such* a great place until the Vorgs arrived."

Matt took a deep breath. He'd gotten away with it—for now.

She sighed and looked down at her folded hands. "They've destroyed life in this city, and all the cities in Gova, in just a couple of months. I'm from the East Side of Bay City. How about you?"

"A long way to the West," said Matt, figuring that he would be safer to pick the opposite end of the city. He realized that keeping up this pretense would not be easy. Should he just be truthful and tell her that he was trapped in his computer game? He dismissed the idea immediately. Even Targon found the idea hard to swallow after all this time. "Targon," he said out loud. "I wonder where he is."

"Who?"

"My friend Targon was with me. Renx, the Vorg who captured you and put me in the materialization chamber, said I'd find him here."

Angel shook her head. "Sometimes they get it wrong. People have disappeared for days and then materialized in really strange places."

"Oh," said Matt. He felt sick for his friend. "Poor Targon. I hope he's okay."

"He's probably better off where he is than here."

Matt's heart quickened. "Really?"

"You don't know a lot about the Vorgs, do you?" said Angel. She frowned and sucked in her cheeks as if trying to figure him out. "I don't know how you could have survived for two months on the run with the little you seem to know. Don't you know *where* this is?"

Matt was stuck. He *didn't* know where they were, so how could he answer otherwise? His heart raced again. How would he get out of this one? He shook his head. "I've been hiding for so long, I don't know a lot about them," he answered.

Angel pursed her lips and scowled. "Gee, I've never met anyone like you before! Every renegade I've come across has survived only because of what they *know* about the Vorgs."

"So what is this place?"

"The Vorgs call it The Factory."

"The factory for what?"

"For turning humans into zombies!" she said in an

angry, haughty tone.

"Zombies?" Matt could not conceal his horror. He thought back to what he had heard the Vorg say to her in the cornfield. Now he understood. He added quickly, "I presume you mean a factory for desensitizing humans and sending them to The Gilded State?"

"Oh, so you do know *something*, then," Angel chuckled. "I was beginning to think you were from another planet." She laughed and tossed back her head.

Matt gulped. "No, I'm from Earth."

"Good to know," she laughed again. "I've had enough with Vorgs. One alien species is enough to deal with."

Matt smiled and breathed deeply once again. So this *was* Earth, at least! Angel had taken his answer as an attempt at a joke. He already liked her. She had a sense of humor even in desperate times. "What's today's date? I've been on the run so long, I've lost track of time."

"June 8th, I think."

"What year?" asked Matt without thinking.

Angel stared at him. "Year?" she repeated. "Now you're really joking, right?"

"I guess I've lost my memory or something," said Matt, not knowing how to explain away his last comment.

"More like they messed your brains up during materialization!" She shook her head. A few red curls bounced over her forehead. She brushed them back. "With the way you're acting, you don't need to go to The Gilded State. You're already there!"

"This has been the weirdest day," said Matt. He laughed with her. "I'm not normally this confused."

She seemed to take pity on him. Her voice softened again. "To answer your question: the Vorgs arrived on the fifth of April 2540, just over two months ago."

Matt's muscles tensed along his spine. He *was* still playing his *Keeper of the Kingdom* game. If this were Earth 2540, he *had* to be playing his game.

Angel continued. "I keep hoping that by some miracle, the Vorgs will leave as suddenly as they arrived, or another empire will come to our aid. Trouble is, everyone is too frightened to help us."

Matt tried to relax. He removed his jacket and laid it on the bench beside him. At least the feeling had returned to every part of his body, but what use was that if he would soon be turned into a zombie? He had to find a way out of here and get his computer back.

He got to his feet and began pacing the room. There wasn't a lot to look at. Apart from the bench there was no furniture, and the window was too high to see out of. A large rectangular grid in the wall at floor level let in air from the outside.

"It's no use looking around—there's no way out," said Angel, anger returning to her voice. "I've paced this room for the last few hours."

"How long do you think we've got here before they turn us into zombies?" asked Matt.

Angel shrugged. "I've no idea. No one I've ever met who's been desensitized is able to talk about what they went through. How about you?"

Matt shook his head and turned away from her gaze as he answered. "No one I've met, either."

"They just walk around in a trance, doing the job they've been given, smiling happily like they've no brain left." Her voice quavered. She sighed and abruptly changed her tone. "They won't do it to me! I've survived two months on the run, and I won't give in now. If only we could get a message to the Resistance."

"The Resistance?" said Matt.

She slapped her forehead and rolled her eyes. "You haven't heard of them, either? Where have you been for the past eight weeks?"

Matt grinned. "Hiding out with my friend. Running from place to place and sleeping in cornfields."

"You're either dead lucky or plain stupid!"

Matt sat on the floor facing her. He ignored her comment. "So, tell me about the Resistance."

She pushed up the torn sleeves of her lacy blouse and leaned forward to talk to him. "The Vorgs took us by surprise. So many came, and we were no match for them. Many Govans gave their lives trying to stop the Vorgs from settling here, but we were defeated." She paused and stared at Matt as if she wanted a sign that he knew at least that much.

Matt nodded and muttered, "Yeah, I know."

The lines across her forehead deepened and her eyes narrowed. "I still can't believe that these disgusting creatures can take a bullet with little injury to their huge bodies *and* can regenerate body parts."

Matt swallowed. Every piece of information about the Vorgs got worse. Regenerate body parts? They seemed to be a formidable enemy. "So who are the Resistance?" Matt asked again.

"When it became obvious that none of our weapons could stop the Vorgs, some people, including scientists, got away. Rumor has it that they used the sewers to escape and have set up a camp on the edge of Gova somewhere near the cliffs. Everyone who manages to escape desensitization tries to join them."

"How do you find the Resistance?"

"I wish I knew." She sighed. "Otherwise I would have been there by now. I'm hoping that our scientists are working on some biological weapon that can destroy them."

"It's early days," said Matt, hoping not to add to her gloom. "Biological weapons can take years to develop, especially if the scientists are away from their laboratories and equipment."

She hung her head. "I know."

Matt heard a fizzing noise behind him. He turned to see Targon splayed on the floor of the materialization chamber.

"Ouch! Where is this place?" he asked, scrambling to his feet and stepping out of the chamber.

"Not any place you want to be!" Angel answered.

"Targon, meet Angel," said Matt, smiling. While he was pleased to see Targon again, he had hoped that his friend might have escaped The Factory.

"Angel? Aren't you the girl that we . . ?"

" . . . heard in the cornfield," Angel finished. "I'm sorry to have the misfortune to meet you." She reached up and shook his hand firmly. "No offense to you or anything, but this isn't a place anyone would want to make a new friend."

"I understand," said Targon. He sat down next to Angel on the bench. "So, what's the plan?"

"Plan?" asked Angel.

"Matt always has a plan," Targon laughed. "Have you worked out how we can get your computer back?"

Matt shrugged. "You're usually the one with brilliant ideas. I hope you can come up with something pretty quickly, or we'll all have scrambled brains."

Chapter 5

Varl could almost touch the sewer grid above his head. The smell of fresh air enticed him up another step.

"Go on, mate," urged Snake. "One more rung and you're there."

"Okay," muttered Varl.

Varl stretched out his right hand to grab the next bar and hauled his body up another foot. Now he had to summon the strength to push open the heavy metal covering of the drain. He took a few deep breaths and placed his palm flat against the iron latticework.

"This one don't slide back—it's on an 'inge," said Snake. "It'll take a bit of effort. Give it a shove upward and let it fall back."

Varl grunted and groaned as he pushed the metal grid up. It hardly made a sound as it fell back on the grassy surface above. He climbed the last two rungs with renewed energy and clambered out, collapsing on his knees in the sunshine.

Snake laughed as he sat on the grass next to him. "Bet you don't wanna do that again in an 'urry, mate!"

Varl chuckled, still panting heavily. "Not likely! I'm getting much too old for these antics."

"Sorry," Snake apologized. "I should've let you rest. Didn't realize how tirin' it would be for someone your age to climb that shaft."

"Just don't tell me we're rock climbing next!" laughed Varl.

Snake was silent. He scrambled to his feet and began collecting a supply of small rocks.

Varl massaged the balls of his cold feet. When the feeling had returned to his toes, he stood up and walked over to join Snake. The grass felt good underfoot. They were on the top of a cliff overlooking a rocky bay. The coast curved in and out for as far as he could see in either direction. He breathed in the fresh sea air, tasting the salt on his tongue, and enjoyed the sun on his face.

Snake threw the stones as far as he could out to sea. Varl peered over the edge. Below was a sheer drop of several hundred feet. The ocean crashed against the rocks below, spraying foam with every wave that came in.

Varl looked at Snake's face and then at the cliffs. He felt suddenly sick. "You're not serious, are you?" he said, realizing that Snake's silence was because he really did have rock climbing in mind.

Snake looked up and grinned. "Sorry, mate. It's the only way you'll be safe from them Vorgs. We've gotta go down."

"Rappelling down a cliff at my age? You've got to be joking!"

"It's not rappellin' exactly. If you don't come down with me, I can't 'elp you, and the Vorgs can get you."

Snake threw the last stone he had collected and started to walk along the edge of the cliff. Varl stood in stunned silence. How much longer should he follow this crazy kid? Did he have any choice?

"You comin', mate?" shouted Snake without looking back.

Varl sighed. If he wanted to outrun the Vorgs and get answers to all of his questions, he had to go.

The strong coastal breeze blew the fine strands of Varl's hair. He followed along the cliff a couple of feet behind the teenager.

Snake stopped minutes later. The path narrowed and the route became treacherous as it veered dangerously close to the edge. He turned away from the cliff and pointed to a mound of earth and stones covered in tall grass.

"Give me an 'and," he said, walking toward a large rock buried in the side of the mound. He tugged at the boulder.

Varl hurriedly joined the boy, and pushed the opposite side of the rock. Together they moved it a few feet, revealing a dug-out hole containing a large plastic box. Snake lifted the container from the pit and took out two small golden cylinders. Each was about a foot long and attached to a network of nylon straps. There were several more cylinders in the box.

Snake handed Varl one of the metal tubes. "'Ere, mate. Put the straps over your shoulders like you'd put on a backpack," he said, demonstrating with his. "Then buckle up the belt."

"What is it?" asked Varl.

"It's a jetpack. These things 'ave been around for years."

Varl turned the smooth cylinder in his hands. It appeared to be hollow at one end, and had no buttons or controls. It gleamed in the brilliant sun.

"How does it work?"

Snake laughed. He reached into the container and tossed Varl a small black box. "'Ere's the controls. The green button turns the jetpack on; the red one turns it off. To go right, press the right arrow; to go left, press the left, and so on. It's easy really."

"How do you hover?" asked Varl, shuddering as he glanced toward the cliff edge.

"To 'over, press the central square."

Varl twisted his face. "I have a feeling I know what's coming next." He put his arms through the shoulder straps and tightened the buckles. "I'll watch you go first."

Snake laughed again. "'Aven't you got any confidence in me yet, mate? It's safe—I promise!"

Varl bit his lip. "If you say so," he said, checking the straps to be sure that they were secure. He wished he could sound more confident. He wasn't seriously going ahead with this madness, was he? Then why had he already put on the jetpack? He knew the answer—and it had nothing to do with his scientific curiosity. The technology wasn't advanced—jetpacks had been around even in 2010, Matt's time period. Varl knew that his boyish sense of adventure had taken over from his common sense. He'd always wanted to try one.

Before he had time to dwell on his fears, Varl heard a loud *whoosh*.   He looked up to see Snake shoot into the air.   He hovered above Varl's head for a few seconds, his feet dancing in the air.   Then he lowered himself slowly to the ground.

"See—it's easy," he grinned.   "You try."

Varl took a deep breath and pressed the green button.   A small red light flickered on the end of the controller.

"Now press the up arrow," urged Snake.

Varl pressed the button.   He shot upward.   He couldn't help but scream with the rush he felt as he soared through the air.

"Quick, press the 'over button!" shouted Snake.

Varl hit the central knob.   He stopped abruptly, suspended in midair.   His stomach turned and he felt dizzy.   *Don't look down*, he told himself.   Was this really happening to him?

"Now, down again!" Snake hollered to him.   "Ease your finger on and off the down arrow, or you'll hit the ground 'ard."

Varl looked out to sea, trying not to think about how high he was.   He attempted to control his descent, but a tiny touch on the button caused him to plummet.   He landed hard, his knees buckling under him.   Snake ran over to him.

"You okay, mate?" he asked, offering Varl his hand.

Varl nodded.   "I'll be fine, I think."   Secretly, he longed to do it again.   He hadn't had that kind of fun in years.

"Okay, we'll do it for real. We've no more time to practice. Let's 'ide the container, just in case them Vorgs come lookin' for you."

"Are they likely to come up here?" asked Varl, helping Snake heave the rock back into position.

"They 'ave done before. We don't know much about them Vorgs—they've only been 'ere for two months. But we do know they don't like the cliffs much. Can't take the risk, though. You may be an 'ot item—if you know what I mean."

Snake checked the area. "Okay, it's as we found it. Let's do it. Follow me. We'll take it nice and slow."

"Right. Do it slowly," muttered Varl.

"Okay, mate. 'Ere we go," said Snake, lifting into the air.

Varl drew in a deep breath, lightly tapping the up arrow this time. He rose more gracefully than he had before and then gently pushed the central square to hover alongside Snake.

"You got it, mate!" Snake beamed. "Now, we're goin' over the edge."

Varl's pulse quickened. There would be no soft landing if he got it wrong this time. He followed Snake over the edge of the cliff. His pants flapped around his legs in the sea breeze. He hovered for a few seconds. The water crashed on the rocks far below. Varl wished that he were calm enough to take in the beauty of the scenery or enjoy the experience, but his heart pumped furiously and he could only think about getting safely down.

"There's Vorgs comin'!" shouted Snake. "Get yourself down and outta sight!"

Varl panicked and pressed the down arrow hard. He felt himself falling fast. The cliff face sped by. The sound of the waves became loud and then louder still. He hit the hover button. Nothing happened. His sweaty thumb hit it hard a second time. Like a bungee jumper, he came to a grinding stop, bouncing upward a few feet before coming to rest perilously close to the rocks below. He was so near to the water that the spray soaked his pants.

Varl sighed with relief. That had been too close. His stomach was a twisted knot. He looked up. Where was Snake? Varl scoured the cliff. He felt a lump in his throat. Surely the boy had not deserted him. Had he fallen to his death?

Varl dismissed the idea. Snake knew what he was doing. He had obviously used the jetpack many times. He looked along the cliff to his right and then to his left. Was there a beach close by to land on?

Varl heard a shrill whistle above the sound of the crashing waves. He looked up again. Snake was kneeling inside a large opening in the cliff face and waving at him madly. Varl shook his head. Now he was hallucinating! There hadn't been an opening in the rocks a few minutes before! Even at the speed he had descended, surely he would have seen a hole *that* size. He looked up again. Snake was definitely there.

Varl pressed very lightly on the up arrow. Staying close to the cliff face, he jetted slowly up to where Snake knelt. Snake stretched out his arm and pulled him into the opening.

"You okay, mate?"

Varl nodded.

"Turn it off," Snake said.

Varl pressed the red button with relief. "Thank goodness," he said, clutching his stomach. He looked out over the sea. "I thought I was about to go to a watery grave."

"Give me the jetpack and move inside," instructed Snake.

Varl stepped into the dark hollow as he fought to undo the straps. Large square panels set into the walls flickered briefly and then brightly lit the area. A faint grating noise made him turn back around. He could no longer hear the sound of waves or see across the ocean. The enormous opening had disappeared and the rock wall appeared solid again. There wasn't any evidence of a door, nor any sign of hinges, cracks or seams. Varl scratched his head.

"Welcome to my 'ome in the cliffs. It's all that is left of the Govan Empire," said Snake. "You'll be safe from the Vorgs 'ere."

Varl looked around in awe. "It's much like my home—I have lived in a cave complex for many years." He wondered if he would ever see the caves of Zaul again.

"Caves?" questioned Snake. He twisted his mouth and tipped his head to one side. "This isn't really a cave."

"No?" replied Varl. He rubbed his hands over the rough walls. "It looks and feels like one to me."

Snake laughed. "I s'ppose you could call it that. But there's one difference. These aren't natural. Govans built the cliff 'omes. They've not been 'ere for millions of years like most caves."

"Oh," said Varl, intrigued.

"Okay, mate," said Snake, hauling Varl to his feet. "Time to show you around."

Snake trotted from the entrance down a narrow tunnel. Varl followed, walking carefully with bare feet on the uneven ground. The walls were smooth and he could see marks left by cutting equipment. He was impressed that under the threat of an invasion, the Govan machinery could create a cave complex like this so quickly. After a short distance, the tunnel expanded into an open area. Other tunnels led off in various directions.

"Sit 'ere," said Snake, pointing to a hard wooden bench. "I'll be back in a minute."

Varl was happy to rest his weary legs, even if it wasn't the most comfortable seat. He looked around the room. It reminded him of the opening hall to his cave complex in Zaul—except that the furnishings in Zaul were colorful and comfortable. Most items in this room were wooden and primitive. They were a far cry from the elaborate buildings and advanced vehicles he had seen in the city.

He heard footsteps and staggered to his feet.

A plump elderly woman, with neat gray hair and a warm smile, waddled into the room. She grasped Varl's hand with both of her own.

"Welcome, Varl. My name is Bee. We're glad that you made it here safely."

"Thank you," said Varl, struggling to free his hand from her strong grip. "It was some journey."

She grinned, a large gap showing between her two front teeth. "It's not an easy one for those of our age. The younger folk leave here daily, at great risk, to collect food and supplies. The scientists are at work in the lab, and the rest of us do what we can to make everyone else as comfortable as possible."

"How did you make this hideaway so quickly, and without the Vorgs' knowledge?" asked Varl.

"We didn't."

"But Snake said these caves were man-made by the Govans."

Bee placed her hands on her hips and laughed. Her cheeks reddened and puffed out. "They were, but not in the last two months. They were built as lookouts two hundred years ago when Bay City and other coastal ports in Gova were under attack."

"Oh, I see," said Varl, feeling somewhat stupid.

She linked her arm through Varl's and led him to the back of the room and down a different tunnel. "Govan technology is quite advanced but our machinery couldn't have performed such a miraculous feat. We moved in when the Vorgs arrived and made changes in a hurry."

Varl nodded. He already liked this jolly woman who was trying to make him feel at home. They came to a wall of rock. Bee dug into a deep pocket in the front of her woolen skirt. She removed a small device resembling the jetpack controls and pointed it at the wall. Varl heard the same grating noise that he had heard earlier, and the rock seemed to melt away, leaving a large opening.

Bee led him into what was obviously the kitchen. A round table sat in the center with a couple of basic wooden stools tucked underneath. Against two walls were several ovens and a deep steel sink with taps. Countless pots and pans, knives and kitchen utensils hung from hooks above the rustic wooden work surfaces. Varl peered through an archway in the far corner, and saw a huge wooden table in the next room. He pulled out one of the kitchen stools and sat in silence, absorbing every detail.

"I know what you're thinking," said Bee.

"You do?"

"You're thinking how primitive everything is here. Everyone who arrives from Bay City is stunned. You'll find that living in the cliff homes will be like taking a trip several hundred years back in time."

"It already does," said Varl, wondering if he should even hint that he was not from Bay City. He guessed from the decorative and elaborate architecture he had seen in the city that the technology there was ahead of what it was here. "At least you've got power and running water in your kitchen."

Bee laughed. "A small compensation for the hardship. But then, this is the price of freedom. I thank my lucky stars every day that I wasn't desensitized and sent to The Gilded State . . ." Her voice trailed off. She sighed and added softly, "Those poor folk. They're walking, brainless shells. Goodness knows how we can save them all and get rid of the Vorgs."

"We'll find a way," said Varl. "It may take time, but there's always a way."

Bee perked up and smiled again. "Now, let's get you something to eat and drink. Then we'll find some accommodation for you—and some shoes."

"Thanks," said Varl. "I'm starving."

He watched her prepare a pot of stew. Smells of steaming vegetables whet his appetite, and his stomach grumbled. He hadn't eaten all day. At least he felt safe from the Vorgs. A sudden chill ran down his spine. He had no idea where Matt and Targon were. He'd been so wrapped up in saving his own neck that he hadn't thought much about them.

"I don't suppose that two young men about Snake's age also found their way here today?" he asked Bee.

She sipped the stew from a large wooden spoon. "Mmm, that's good," she murmured, turning around from the stove. "No, you're the only one to arrive in days. Why, were you with friends?"

Varl nodded. "We got separated."

He didn't know how he could begin to explain that he, like Bee, was a character caught up in Matt's computer game. He wondered if he *really* believed it himself. He shuddered. What if Matt and Targon hadn't been so fortunate? What if they had been caught by the Vorgs, desensitized and turned into zombies? Without Matt and his computer, Varl was stuck here. Without Matt, he would live with the Govans in the cliff homes for the rest of his days . . . that is, if the Vorgs didn't catch him.

Chapter 6

The early morning sun filtered into the prison cell through the tiny window. Matt hadn't slept. He lay on his stomach, looking through the meshed air vent in the bottom of the wall. He could see grass on the other side. He felt around the edge of the grid, but found no screws or bolts. It was firmly plastered into the bricks.

"I've already checked that out," said Angel, standing over him. "It won't budge."

"Could we chip away at the plaster and loosen it?" suggested Matt.

"With what?" asked Targon. "Besides, I doubt any of us could squeeze through a hole that narrow."

"I've seen it done in old war movies," said Matt, scrambling to his feet. He brushed the brick dust off his hands. "If we could remove the grid, we could chip away the mortar from between the bricks, remove them, and make the hole bigger."

"How are you going to do that without any tools?" asked Targon. "There's nothing in this room but the bench, and you'd need something sharp."

"Like the pointed ends of my earrings?" Angel asked. She removed one of the golden loops and flashed the sharp post in front of Matt's eyes.

Matt smiled. "Thanks, Angel, but I think it would take

ages to chip plaster using those, and they're so thin they'd probably bend."

She sighed and put the shiny loop back in her ear.

"So, is *that* it?" asked Targon. "*That's* the best idea we've got to get us out of here?"

"Unless you can think of anything better," said Matt. He walked clumsily over to the bench and flopped down on the hard surface.

Targon sat next to him. He leaned over and put his head in his hands. "I think we're about to get desensitized."

"No, we're not!" shouted Angel. She shoved her hands deep into her pockets and stared at Matt with a determined expression. "There has to be something else we can do."

"We wouldn't be able to overpower even *one* Vorg without getting a dose of venom," replied Matt.

"What do we know about Vorgs?" asked Targon.

"None of the Govan guns or lasers work on them," Angel explained. "The creatures are stunned for a few seconds and then regenerate their body parts."

Targon gulped. "*We* don't have any weapons anyway."

The door hummed and it began to slide open.

"We're out of time," said Matt. He got to his feet and stood next to Angel. "It'll be okay. We'll think of something."

"Who are you kidding?" Angel replied.

Matt's stomach churned. Angel was being realistic.

Who was he trying to convince? Only himself. They had just minutes to escape before the Vorgs took control of their brains.

A Vorg stood in the open doorway. "This way," he directed.

Matt recognized the husky voice of Renx even if he could hardly tell the creatures apart by their looks. He hesitated, racing through his options. But there weren't any. If he refused to go, Renx would give him another dose of venom. The Vorg had warned that a second dose might kill him. At best he would be paralyzed and have no chance of defending himself. Matt thought better of arguing and slowly led the way into the corridor. Targon and Angel followed.

Several humans were assembled in a long line. Some seemed anxious, others calm and accepting of their fate in The Gilded State. Another Vorg stood watching them from a distance.

"Go to the end of the line," hissed Renx. "Get ready to remove your shoes."

Matt stood behind the last person. He looked down at his Nikes. His heart pounded. Desensitization was getting too close. There had to be something he could do. He looked around to see if there was any way to escape. There were no windows or doors, and there was nowhere to hide. A narrow staircase wound upward on his left. Renx stood directly in front of the bottom step, blocking any chance of escape. Besides, where did it lead? For all Matt knew, a dozen more Vorgs could be waiting at the top. The floor was concrete, and the metal struts, which ran up the walls to support the ceiling, were no more than ten feet tall. If he tried to climb up to get out of danger, as he had in the past, any eight-foot Vorg would pluck him off the beam with ease.

As he weighed his options, a heated discussion took place at the front of the line and two men began pushing each other. Matt strained to see above the heads of the rest of the humans. A tall woman entered the argument. Renx marched to the front of the line and ordered them to cease. The woman yanked a silver canister from its holder on the wall.

"You'll not take me, you ugly brutes!" she hollered, and aimed the canister at Renx's face.

Matt watched her spray the contents directly at the stunned Vorg. At the sound of a pressurized liquid bursting free, the men stopped fighting. Matt covered his nose as an acrid smell filled the corridor. A steamy purple mist rose to the ceiling.

Renx yelled in agony. "My eyes! My eyes! Get the humans under control!" He scratched at his face with his claws.

Matt watched the fracas. Everyone was engrossed in the struggle. Renx continued to rub his eyes. The other Vorg was lashing out with his tongue at the woman holding the canister. This was their opportunity. Matt sidled away from the line. He faced Targon and pointed toward the stairs.

"Let's go!" he whispered to Angel.

Matt sprinted up the stairs after Targon, Angel close on his heels. The plain concrete walls were monotonous with no railings, and the steps, narrow. Matt knew that if he lost his concentration it would be easy to slip. The stairs seemed to rise forever, spiraling upward. He focused on putting one foot quickly after the other.

Targon slowed down.

"Keep going!" urged Matt, attempting to take two steps at a time.

They came to the top of the stairs and entered a hallway.

Targon peered around the corner. "It's all clear. Which way?" he gasped.

Shouts came from below. Heavy feet resounded on the stairs.

"They've realized we've escaped," said Matt. "They're coming. Either way, Targon—just go!"

Targon turned to the right, and Matt and Angel followed. Three Vorgs in the distance shouted a warning and began running toward them.

"More Vorgs!" shouted Targon. "And I think they're armed."

"He's right!" said Angel. "They've got jazooks! Now we're in trouble."

"Go up again!" bellowed Matt, pointing to another staircase on their right. "It'll buy us time. The Vorgs have enormous feet—the narrow steps are hard enough for us."

Matt saw the Vorgs raise their polished black

weapons and take aim. He leaped up the stairs. His mouth felt dry. His legs ached with every step. Fear and adrenaline pushed him on. The racket of numerous pairs of hefty feet echoed from below. Every second counted.

"Faster," Matt urged.

Angel began wheezing. "Don't think I can."

Bright sun streamed into the stairwell. The top was in sight.

"We're nearly there," panted Matt. "We can do it."

"We're on the roof!" shouted Targon as he reached the last step. "Where can we go? We're trapped!"

Matt stopped and surveyed the flat roof. On his left were three large domed storage sheds. There were red markings on the ground, which reminded him of the medivac landing pads on hospital roofs back home.

"Look over there . . . parked in the far corner!" shouted Angel. "It's an airbug!"

Matt and Targon raced side by side across the flat roof after Angel.

She turned her head and screamed, "Run! The Vorgs are at the top of the stairs!"

Matt heard something whiz past his left ear and saw a yellow dart rebound off the side of the airbug. "Faster! They're firing darts at us!"

Angel ran around the back of the airbug and dived into the pilot's seat. "Get in!" She switched on the engines.

Matt scrambled in next to her. Targon threw himself into the cockpit as more darts were fired.

"Angel, close the door," he shouted.

"There isn't one," Angel yelled above the whirring of the engines.

The whoosh of air caught Matt by surprise. They jerked upward a few feet and then a few feet more. Targon gripped his seat, nervously looking at the open-sided cockpit.

"Can you drive this thing?" asked Matt.

"Sure," said Angel, lifting them higher. "Done it hundreds of times before."

"Then get us in the air," Matt begged. He flinched as darts pinged against the side of the airbug. "The Vorgs are closing in."

"Don't worry, their jazooks can't bring down one of these craft."

"But they can hit *us!*" said Targon, moving in as far as he could from the open side.

"The darts fired by the jazooks are filled with Vorgs' venom, so four times out of five you'll only be paralyzed if you're hit," Angel responded.

"Great," muttered Targon. "What about the fifth time?"

They suddenly lurched upward and over the edge of the building. Angel clutched the wheel and clenched her teeth.

Matt felt a wave of relief, and then sudden fear as the craft seemed to dive toward the ground.

"Angel, pull it up!"

She pulled back hard on the wheel, causing the

airbug to tip and sway. Matt clung to the dashboard. After what seemed like minutes, the craft leveled.

Matt sat back in his seat, his heart still racing. He threw Angel an annoyed look. "I thought you said you'd driven one of these loads of times before."

"I have—in my virtual airbug game." She smiled.

Matt gasped, horrorstruck. "A computer game?"

She nodded. "I'm pretty good at flying . . . usually win the race."

"I can't believe you lied to us!" said Matt. He opened his mouth to reprimand her some more, but she snapped back at him.

"You wouldn't have got in if I'd told you I'd never driven an airbug for real. We didn't have any choice."

Matt said no more. She was right, of course.

"How safe are we?" Targon asked, worry in his voice.

"We're not," replied Angel. "They'll have airbugs looking for us within minutes."

Matt looked at the dashboard, which appeared to be one huge video screen. "How easy is it for them to locate us? Any tracking device on this thing?"

Angel shook her head. "Airbugs are a Govan vehicle. Most airbugs were privately owned before the Vorgs arrived in their more sophisticated spacecraft. They took them from us for local transportation. Each bug has a radio and an onboard computer, but no tracking device. We don't need clearance from air traffic control because bugs don't fly above 1,000 feet and they're not allowed near the spaceport."

"Great," said Matt. He ignored the word spaceport. Right now he had too many other questions. "If the Vorgs can locate us only by sight, and there were no other airbugs on the roof, that should give us a little time."

"Five minutes' head start, no more. We've got to come up with something good."

"Any suggestions?" asked Targon.

"I know of one place that might do as a temporary hideout. I just need to work out how to set this computer so I can use auto pilot." She touched the screen in several places and selected speed and coordinates. "Now you can sit back and enjoy the ride. We're already out of Bay City." She folded her hands in her lap.

Matt grinned. They were flying smoothly, and his heart wasn't pumping quite so furiously, but he could hardly relax and enjoy the view with Angel at the controls!

* * * * *

Jesper of the Mount was tired and worried. The day had started badly. How would he explain the escape of an old man and three young Govans from The Factory in two days?

He straightened his vest and smoothed out the creases in his leather pants. This meeting would not be easy. Gubala, Great Leader of the Vorgs, had little patience for those who failed. To be Commander of The Factory was a prized position of responsibility. Right from the beginning, as soon as the advance party had arrived in Gova, Gubala had entrusted him with the job of desensitizing humans. Jesper knew that four escapes would be a serious mark against him.

Yorak of the Vale and Harless of the Waters were waiting for him to make a mistake. Both of his rivals would jump at the chance to take over running The Factory. He would not allow that to happen. He thought about how he might best approach Gubala. Should he be honest with the Great Leader and admit his error, or should he find an excuse and someone to blame?

Jesper picked up his thick purple cloak. The rich color was an emblem of his superiority as a leader and a reminder of his home. He was Jesper of the Mount, a respected leader from the Purple Mountains of Vorgus. He was proud of his heritage. He would not fail in his position of authority and bring disrespect to his family.

Jesper draped the long garment over his right shoulder. The day was too hot to wear an outer garment, but it was convention that when meeting with the Great Leader, an officer of the state must be dressed appropriately. He decided that he would have to put it on before entering the Great Complex.

The Govan mirror on his office wall was too low for an eight-foot Vorg. He grunted as he bent his head to look at himself. Govan beds were too small, ceilings too low and everything here was generally unsatisfactory. He hated the tiny airbugs and even more, the Govan architecture.

"Fancy, cramped designs," he muttered. "I'll be glad when Vorgs are totally in control. Then we can construct buildings to our own requirements."

He knew that would not happen until his advance party had succeeded in wiping out the Resistance, and had rounded up every last Govan renegade. Only then would Gubala, the Great Leader, allow millions of Vorgs to move to Earth. It had to be done quickly. Vorgus was on a collision course with Galatin 4. Everyone needed to be evacuated.

He smiled as he imagined the sky above Bay City black with arriving Vorg spacecraft. "That will be a great day," he said to his reflection. "One after another they'll come, hour after hour, day after day. We'll start with this little Empire and colonize the entire planet Earth bit by bit. We will be remembered as the saviors of the Vorg species!"

Chapter 7

Matt looked out the windshield for the first time. From the air, the Govan Empire had a beauty that he had not appreciated from the ground. The green fields of corn mixed with the purples and yellows of other crops created a pretty patchwork of color. In the distance, specks of white seemed to dance on a blue background. His first thought was that the cloud formations were different here. Then Matt realized that he was looking at the ocean—the waves cresting as they rolled into shore. Bay City was near the coast.

Angel reverted to manual controls. She allowed the airbug to drop several hundred feet and began circling close to the ground.

"Where are we?" asked Matt.

"Close to the graveyard," she replied.

Targon grimaced. "The what?"

"Just hold your tongue and wait and see!" she snapped.

"Excuse me for asking!" retorted Targon. He sat back in silence.

Matt looked at Targon's puzzled face and then closely at Angel. It was unlike her to give such a harsh reply. She had snapped at both of them before, but not in a mean way—just out of frustration. She stared ahead through the windshield, eyes as wide as a cat's at night, and lips pursed tightly together. Matt had not seen this side of her. She had seemed fearless, constantly joking in spite of their grim situation. Now she appeared to grip the wheel in deep concentration. They circled again. Matt looked below. They had definitely been over this terrain several times before. He recognized a field in which hundreds of airbugs of all colors were parked in rows. It seemed a strange thing to see in the midst of fields of wheat.

"Angel, we've flown over here before. Is there a problem?" he asked her gently.

She shook her head.

"Then why aren't we flying on or putting down?"

She didn't reply.

"Angel, talk to me, please," begged Matt. "You're beginning to scare me. I can tell something's wrong. Has the airbug got problems?"

"I . . . I've . . . I've never landed an airbug before," Angel stammered.

"What?" said Targon. His jaw dropped.

Matt looked from Targon to Angel. His stomach tightened. "I thought you said you usually won the race in your virtual airbug game."

"I did. But the race always ended when I flew over the finish line. I never had to land one of these things!"

Matt gulped. "Do you *know* how to get us down?"

"I can guess," she replied.

"Okay," said Matt taking deep breaths. He tried to

remain calm and clear his head. "Let's think carefully. What should we do first?"

"I think we should go back on autopilot," said Angel.

"Right . . . but keep us circling at this level," added Matt.

Angel did as Matt instructed. Matt looked at the computer screen in front of them. It had to be like any other computer, right? Couldn't these things land themselves? His heart pounded. He pulled up the menu and the various options. In bold red letters, third on the list, he read, *"Landing."* Matt pressed the square. Several blank boxes faced him. He needed to fill in information.

"Can you work out the landing coordinates?" asked Matt.

Angel nodded and pulled up a map on her half of the huge screen. She then set a grid over the top and finally came up with two sets of figures.

Matt keyed in the numbers. "Great, Angel. We're doing great." Secretly his stomach was churning and he had serious doubts about how they would get down. "Now give me our current height and the speed you think we will need to descend at."

After keying in the numbers Angel gave him, Matt scrolled down and pressed a small box in the bottom right of the screen, *Proceed with Landing.* Matt's hands trembled. There would be no going back. He touched the colored square. Bright blue letters, *Landing Pattern Commencing,* flashed on the screen.

"Hold tight, everyone," said Matt. "We're going down."

Before he could finish his words, the craft began to dive toward the field full of parked airbugs. Instead of slowing, they seemed to be gaining speed as they neared the ground.

"We're too fast!" screamed Angel. "Abort the landing!"

With shaking hands Matt reached for the screen and pulled up the options. His head spun as he quickly skimmed the choices.

"There it is, *Revert to Manual*," read Angel. "I've got the wheel. Do it! Quick!"

Matt's fingers aimed for the square. The increasing speed made it difficult for him to reach forward and aim for the correct place.

"Zang it!" shouted Targon. "We're nearly in the trees!"

Matt stretched out his arm. He lunged for the screen and hit the square. *Manual* flashed in huge red letters. Angel pulled back on the wheel. The airbug hissed as the extra thrust lifted them up, skirting the treetops. They soared back into the sky.

"Whew! That was close," said Angel, exhaling deeply. "Everyone okay?"

Matt felt like throwing up. The experience had brought him close to death yet again. His ears felt like they were burning all the way down his ear canals to his brain. He wondered how much more excitement his heart could take. His hands still shook. He placed them on his knees in an effort to calm himself. Targon was white. He sat in silence staring through the windshield.

"Now what?" asked Angel. "Do you want to try again at a slower speed?"

Matt shook his head. "It's obvious that we can't guess at the figures."

"You're saying it's up to me then?" Her voice trembled noticeably.

Matt nodded. "I think it's our best option. At least you've got a feel for how this craft handles. Targon, what's your vote?"

Targon turned his head slowly to look at Matt. "I've got more confidence in Angel than in autopilot," he said with a glazed expression.

"Okay," said Matt. He sighed. "That settles it. We've both got confidence in you. You've got us this far. You can do it. Just take your time."

Angel drew in several deep breaths. She cut the engine speed, pushed the wheel forward slightly and tipped the nose down.

"We need to be about twenty feet above where we want to land, and then the bug will hover and put down horizontally."

"So far, so good. The craft speed seems reasonable," said Matt, trying to remain calm and focused. "What are we aiming for?"

"The graveyard," replied Angel. "We got the location right last time—but not the speed." She took her right hand off the wheel and pointed through the windshield. "The airbug graveyard is where all the old airbugs are brought before they're dismantled for spares and recycling."

Matt smiled. Now he understood why hundreds of different colored airbugs were parked in the middle of farmland.

"Look for a space at the end of one of the rows," said Angel as they approached.

"You're still too fast," said Matt. His heart quickened. If Angel wasn't careful, their airbug would end up a smashed wreck like some of those parked below.

Angel cut the speed and pulled the bug level. The field was suddenly under them and then, just as suddenly, gone.

"Zang it!" said Matt, echoing Targon's familiar expression. "We've missed it. You'll have to try again. Can we stay at this height and circle around?"

"I'll try," she replied, turning the vehicle. "I'll attempt to come in from this side."

Matt swallowed hard. "You're doing just great," he encouraged.

"I saw a space at the end of the far row," said Targon.

Angel slowed the craft to a virtual stop as they approached the field a second time. They crawled over the top of thousands of airbugs laying waste in the scorching sun.

"There's the space," said Targon excitedly.

Matt watched him point through the windshield with dramatic arm movements and then slump back in his seat as if his nervousness had returned.

Angel guided them slowly across the field. "Here goes," she announced. "I'm cutting the engines completely."

"Let's hope we don't fall the last twenty feet," muttered Targon.

"Thanks for the vote of confidence," Angel snapped.

The high-pitched whirring of the airbug stopped. Matt held his breath. He listened, frozen in his seat. Then the deafening sound of rushing air allowed him to breathe easy.

Angel lowered the silver airbug carefully between two red ones. She beamed at Matt when the craft touched the ground. Matt felt a slight shudder under his seat as the engines shut down.

They sat in silence for a few seconds. Matt gathered his thoughts and felt thankful for yet another escape from a dangerous situation.

"Thanks, Angel," he said. "I knew you could do it."

"No, you didn't!" she retorted. "Admit it, you had your doubts for a while there."

Matt smiled. "Okay, I admit it. But really, thanks. You saved our lives."

She gave him a smug grin. "No thanks necessary—just glad you enjoyed the ride!"

"Matt's right," said Targon. "Thanks to you, we'll all live to see another day." He leaned across Matt and shook her hand.

Angel sat upright. "We'd better start thinking about our next move. We haven't got time to sit here. The Vorgs will be searching the empire for us."

"Well, this smart move of yours will buy us time," congratulated Matt. "From the air they won't be able to pick out this airbug from the others."

"No, but the Vorgs aren't stupid, either," said Angel. "They'll work it out. We'd just better be gone by the time they do!"

* * * * *

Varl snuggled under the heavy blanket. The cliff homes weren't the most comfortable accommodation. The temperature in the caves was cool and the walls felt damp. But at least he was safe from the Vorgs. Because there were no windows, it felt like the middle of the night. Varl's watch said otherwise. He knew he had to get up.

Bee had given him a small room with a narrow bed in one corner and a tall chest of drawers in another. She had said that breakfast was at eight. It was already 7:55. Varl swung his legs over the edge of the bed and picked the green pants off the floor where he'd thrown them the night before. He slipped into a pair of shoes that Bee had given him, and pulled the rounded neck of the green top over his head. He wondered what had happened to the old man who had traded clothes with him. He might never know.

Varl smoothed down his hair, picked up the small controller he had been given by Bee and walked over to the door. He chuckled. At least this technology was more advanced than everything else in the cliff homes. He held the device up to a small recess in the wet rock. As if by magic, the solid wall melted away to reveal an opening.

He wandered down the corridor following the sound of a mellow voice and the smell of food. He couldn't decide what was being served for breakfast—not one of the sweet smells was familiar. The door to the kitchen was open. Varl peered around the wall to see Bee standing over the stove. She stopped singing and smiled when she saw him.

"Morning. I trust you slept well?"

Varl nodded. "Thank you, I did."

"Breakfast is about ready. Come, I'd like you to meet those who live in B Family of the cliff homes."

"*B* Family?" queried Varl.

"We divided into groups or families of between six and twelve people for ease of cooking and sleeping. Most of the people in each family aren't related by blood. Many of us lost our real relatives to the Vorgs. But we support each other here like a family would." She linked her arm through Varl's and led him into the dining room.

A large rectangular table was set for breakfast. Two people sat on either side, and an elderly man sat in one of the heavy end chairs. Varl smiled at the five individuals waiting to greet him. It was only Snake that he recognized.

Snake scrambled to his feet. "Mornin', mate. I 'ope you've recovered."

"Yes, I have, thanks. That was quite a journey you took me on yesterday, but I was in good hands."

"Glad you thought so. I'll introduce everyone else," said Snake. He walked to the end of the table and rested his hands squarely on the shoulders of the older man. "This 'ere is Doc."

"Pleased to meet you, Varl," said Doc, peering at him over his gold-rimmed glasses. "I'm the one who can supposedly cure all your ills. I do my best with limited drugs and supplies, and my arthritic fingers, of course."

Varl laughed. "I can see, Doc, that we have something in common." He raised his hands and wiggled his swollen joints.

Doc smiled. "See me afterward. I've just the thing for you."

Snake walked on to the next person round the table. He tapped the head of a young lady with gleaming jet-black hair. "And this 'ere is Spider."

"Spider?" asked Varl.

Snake laughed. "It's not what you think, mate."

Spider got to her feet. "Welcome, Varl. It's nothing to do with the black hair, and I guarantee I don't bite." She grinned. "I'm the creative one. I spin and sew wonderful garments from the strangest of materials."

"Oh, now I see," said Varl. He bit his lip, wondering if he dared to ask her for help so soon. "Don't suppose there's any chance of some new clothes? These aren't exactly comfortable . . . or to my taste."

"I'll see what I can do," Spider said with a huge smile.

Snake moved along to the next person. "This 'ere is Fly."

The young man was in his late teens, Varl guessed. His hair had been shaved off except for a narrow strip of curls that ran along the top of his head and down to the nape of his neck.

"Fly?" questioned Varl. "Named for a similar reason to Snake?"

"You're catching on," Fly replied. "There's no one who can use a jetpack like me. I can be in and out of here before you've blinked!"

Varl laughed. "Hope you'll show me how!"

"I'd be delighted," replied Fly.

Snake walked around the end of the table to the person who had sat next to him. "This 'ere is Chip."

Varl studied the middle-aged man, deciding that he must be in his late forties. Chip was balding, and he had a dark brown mustache that curled down to his chin. "Let me guess," said Varl, enjoying the game. "Chip as in microchip?"

Chip nodded. "Indeed. I'm the technology expert amongst us. There are several other scientists in the cliff homes. Together we are trying to find a way to destroy the Vorgs."

Snake sat down next to Chip and gestured to Varl. "Take a seat, mate. Tell us what you do and 'ow you escaped them Vorgs before I found you."

Varl sat down on the other side of Chip. "Thank you all for making me so welcome. I'm also a scientist, although where I come from the technology is very different, I believe." Varl paused. He realized that he had just created a whole load of trouble for himself. But what else could he say? It would soon be obvious that he wasn't from Gova.

Bee brought in a large plate stacked high with steaming food.

"Pancakes, Varl," she said, putting them down on the table. "They're good, I promise." She sat at the other end in the empty chair. "I heard what you said as I came in. So where are you from, if not from Gova?"

It was the question that Varl had been dreading. He studied the six people at the table. No one reached for food. They all stared at him.

Varl looked at Chip. Would the true explanation be accepted? Who was he kidding? Did Varl even believe it himself? Besides, Matt wasn't here with his computer. Explaining that they were all trapped in a boy's computer game wasn't the way to be accepted by his new family. He would have to use the excuse he had used before—time travel. After all, time travel had been a possibility for hundreds of years.

Varl grinned nervously. "I'm hoping that you are significantly advanced in your technology here in Gova that you will believe what I'm about to tell you." He looked straight at Chip. "I'm sure that you, of all people, will examine the possibility before you condemn me."

Chip bristled as if preparing to hear something outlandish. "Go ahead," he said in a forthright manner. "I'm listening."

Varl swallowed. "I'm a time traveler. I come from a place called the Kingdom of Zaul. I had two young men traveling with me, but I don't know what has happened to them."

The room was quiet, but Varl sensed that his comments had been accepted. Everyone smiled and began reaching for pancakes.

Chip chuckled and patted him on the hand. "Varl, you needn't have worried. Everyone in this room has time traveled at least once before."

"Indeed?" said Varl, quite taken aback.

Chip tucked into a pancake and continued to talk with his mouth full. "Although, since the arrival of the Vorgs and the loss of our time machines, it has been out of the question."

Varl knew that it was possible to travel forwards or backwards in time, but technology in Zaul had *not* developed that far. "I would be interested to learn more about your methods," he added as calmly as he could. Inside, he could hardly quell his excitement.

"And I from you. What time period are you from?" Chip asked, filling his mouth.

"2540," replied Varl, helping himself to food.

Everyone else laughed.

Chip stopped chewing, swallowed his mouthful, and

rested his fork on his plate. "Really?" he chuckled.

Varl felt uneasy. "Is something funny?" he asked.

"This is also the year 2540," replied Chip. "I don't think you have traveled very far this time." The others laughed again.

Varl nearly choked on his pancake. "2540?"

"With all of Earth's small kingdoms and empires constantly at war, it is quite probable that you had never heard of the Empire of Gova," said Chip.

Varl felt sick. *Empire of Gova?* Yet again the facts supported what Matt had always claimed. Varl was beginning to realize that he could no longer deny the truth. He *was* a character in the boy's computer game and this was the third level, *Keeper of the Empire*. He really did have to find Matt and Targon as fast as possible.

Chapter 8

Jesper of the Mount parked his airbug outside the Great Complex and stepped into the sun. It was another scorching day. He threw his cloak around his shoulders, complaining bitterly as he struggled with the clasp under his chin. Clasps, zippers and fasteners were never easy for a Vorg's huge hands and sharp claws to manipulate.

He looked up at the concrete building in front of him. Vorgs had hurriedly built the Great Complex as their new center of operations immediately after their arrival. It was plain but practical, and nothing like the flamboyant Govan architecture that he detested.

Jesper puffed out his massive chest and lumbered up the ramp. He was not looking forward to his meeting with Gubala. The Great Leader had a temper. Still, Jesper felt confident. The Great Leader had praised his efforts the week before and would surely overlook his first mistake as Commander of The Factory.

He smiled as he entered the foyer. It would be wonderful not to have to climb steps, squeeze into revolving doors or bend his head under low Govan ceilings for the next couple of hours.

He stood on the grid in the foyer while the scanner searched for weapons and checked his identity. When a synthetic voice announced that he was clear to proceed, he walked through the opening door into a materialization chamber. A quicker way to travel, he thought, but not a process he enjoyed. He pressed #6 on the menu. The glass door closed. His heavy boots disappeared first.

Jesper arrived on Level Six directly outside Gubala's office. He checked to see that he was intact before stepping out of the chamber, even though he had been materialized thousands of times before. He had a deep fear that one day he would arrive at a destination minus an arm or a leg.

Yorak of the Vale swept out of Gubala's office. His dark green cloak signified his superior rank and control of the Green Valleys of Vorgus. Yorak's cloak was covered in a layer of dust. Jesper felt pleased. Gubala liked his Commanders of State to look well groomed, but Yorak looked dirty.

Jesper decided to be courteous, even though he despised him. "Morning, Yorak. It has been a while since we have spoken. Have you located the Resistance?"

"I hear you have been kept busy, Jesper," Yorak scoffed, ignoring his question. "You are the talk of all Vorgs. Humans are stupid and yet they seem to have outwitted you twice in two days!" The heavy folds of leathery skin under his chin wobbled as he laughed.

"Every new job takes time to learn. Humans are not stupid," Jesper declared.

Yorak sneered. "They are, from what I've seen. I don't know why we are even bothering to search for the

Resistance. Their numbers are so small, the group is insignificant."

"Most humans are just frightened and intimidated by us, but there are some who are capable of an organized rebellion. I'm sure you will discover that for yourself in due course," replied Jesper.

"Colonizing the Earth is going to be *too* easy," Yorak hissed. His eyes narrowed, and he added in a sinister tone, "I should watch your back. There are many who would prize your position."

"You included?" Jesper asked.

Yorak grinned and went on his way.

Jesper boiled with rage. How easy it was to criticize someone when you knew nothing of a job or its problems. Yorak was a pompous idiot. His overconfidence and underestimation of the Govan Resistance would be his downfall.

The double doors to the Great Leader's Chamber were open. Jesper entered and walked across the room to where Gubala sat with his back to the door, looking out the window. Three long spikes that protruded from the base of the leader's skull were visible above the top of the leather chair. Gubala swiveled around and looked Jesper in the eyes.

"You're late," he said without expression.

Jesper glanced at the timepiece on Gubala's desk. He was one minute early. This was not going well, and he hadn't even said a word.

"I apologize, Great Leader. The scanner at the

entrance took longer than I had anticipated."

"Save your excuses for when you need them," said Gubala. He leaned forward across the desk and hissed, "I think you've got some *real* explaining to do."

"Humans are not as stupid as every Vorg seems to believe," Jesper began. "They can be cunning, devious and intelligent."

Gubala tapped his long claws on the desk. "Vorgs are a superior race with more advanced technology. We have easily colonized other planets where the native species has proved far more of a challenge. I have seen nothing in the last two months that would indicate humans might be a problem for us."

"I fear that we underestimate their ability, Great Leader."

"*You* underestimated their ability," Gubala snapped. "No other Vorg in a commanding position has had one escape. You have lost four humans in two days!"

Jesper stood tall. "It will not happen again, Great Leader. We will be more careful at The Factory."

Gubala hissed. He lowered his voice. "You're right, it will not happen again. You are relieved of your position!"

Jesper's lower jaw dropped. "But, Great Leader . . ."

"There is no further discussion. You will be given another assignment. Take three days' leave and then report back."

Jesper of the Mount was stunned. He stood motionless for a few seconds, staring at Gubala. The

Great Leader swiveled his chair toward the window. Jesper knew that was his cue to leave. If he continued to argue, his next assignment would be a menial task. Already he had brought disrespect to his family in the Purple Mountains. Reluctantly he headed for the door.

Harless of the Waters greeted Jesper in the corridor. He draped the bottom of his royal blue cape over his right arm and gave Jesper a knowing smile.

"Bad day?" Harless asked, almost breaking into a laugh.

Jesper snorted his response. "It seems you've heard."

"I am to replace you." Harless grinned.

"But I've only just left Gubala's office," said Jesper. "So how could you possibly have . . . ?"

"He called me this morning. Mistakes like yours are not tolerated—you know that!"

Jesper snapped his teeth together in anger. Gubala had made up his mind before talking to him.

"Good luck to you, Harless," Jesper hissed. "You'll need it!"

* * * * *

Matt sat in the airbug wondering what they should do next. He needed to find his computer. How could he convince Angel to go along with them without telling her the real story?

"Could we still use this airbug if we traded its registration plate with one from another bug?" asked

Matt.

Angel gasped. "You want me to pilot this thing a second time?"

"Just a thought," said Matt. "We'd get farther away from here in a bug than on foot."

"True." Angel was quiet for a minute. "I don't think the Vorgs have had time to set up any kind of airbug tracking system. Since Govans destroyed most of the computer files during the invasion, the Vorgs won't know which bugs are still in use and which aren't. So, yes it's possible."

"And they'll be looking for the registration plate on this one, right?" asked Targon.

Angel nodded. "It's all they'll have to go on. There are thousands of silver airbugs."

"So let's do it!" said Matt eagerly.

"It's a good idea but it's not that easy. Most plates are taken off the airbugs when they come to the graveyard. The owners then put them on the new vehicle."

"Oh," said Matt, feeling glum. "So there may not be another plate to exchange ours with."

"We might get lucky and find a couple of plates. If the owner isn't buying a new airbug then the plate stays on the old one."

"I'll start looking while you and Matt remove the plate from this one," said Targon.

Angel's face brightened. "Okay, let's get to work. We'll need tools to remove the fasteners."

Matt followed her to the back of the bug.

She studied the plate. "Standard Govan fasteners."

Matt fingered the tiny gold triangular pins, wondering how to remove them.

"We need to find a spiral," said Angel, as if she were reading his thoughts. "Most tool kits will have one."

"Is there likely to be a tool kit in the back?" asked Matt.

"Probably," said Angel. "I can open the rear door, but the controls are in the front. I'll be right back."

Matt scrambled inside before the door had completely risen. He looked around but could see nothing resembling a toolbox.

"Lift the floor panel," instructed Angel when she returned. "Tools are usually kept in the well underneath."

Matt lifted the lid. He smiled when he saw a large collection of tools. He rifled through the assortment until he found what he thought was a spiral.

"This it?" he asked Angel.

"Right tool, wrong attachment," she answered. "It needs to have the triangular head."

Matt ferreted around, located the tiny end piece and crawled back to the door. He handed her the parts. Angel connected them together and set to work. The tiny device spun into action. The fasteners sprung from the holes and the plate fell on the grass.

"That was quick," said Matt.

"I used to help my dad in his workshop . . . " Angel swallowed hard.

"I'm sorry," said Matt, sensing her pain. "You must miss your family." *Like I miss mine*, he thought.

Angel didn't answer. She shrugged and brushed back a strand of hair from her eyes. Matt wondered if she ever allowed her tough exterior to soften.

She stood up and looked around. "Okay. Now we need to take a plate off another bug. Let's hope Targon found one."

Matt heard a whirring noise. "An airbug's approaching!" he shouted in panic.

"Hide!" shouted Angel, grabbing the loose plate and the spiral off the grass. "Get on the floor of the airbug . . . quick!"

Matt gulped. "But what about Targon?"

Angel lowered the back door and dragged Matt by the sleeve into the open front of the silver bug. "There's no time to warn him . . . he's on his own. Let's hope he heard it approaching. Lie on the floor . . . now!"

Matt lay still, facing the open side. The airbug was cramped with two of them in the cockpit under the control panel and computer system. He tried to reassure himself that as long as the Vorgs didn't land, and as long as Targon was out of sight, they'd be fine.

The whirring engines grew loud and then slowed. Matt watched the grass in front of him blow wildly. The airbug stopped directly above, not far off the ground. His heart pounded in his ear canals. He swallowed hard. Would the Vorgs land?

"They're hovering above," he whispered to Angel.

"Don't worry. They're just checking. Unless they see movement they won't land. There's no heat-seeking equipment on commercial airbugs so they can't tell we're here."

"What if that's not a commercial airbug?"

"It is. The military bugs are much bigger and have a different sound. Govans didn't have many. Vorg leaders commandeered all of them. A regular Vorg patrol won't have one."

Matt was still worried even though Angel sounded so confident. He prayed that Targon had heard the approaching bug in time and had stayed where he was. Time seemed to drag. Matt strained to see his watch. They had been on the floor for only a few minutes but it felt like hours.

The sound of rushing air and whirring engines began to fade. The grass stood still again. They had been lucky. Matt began to move, but Angel grabbed his jacket and made him wait several minutes before she allowed him to leave the cockpit.

Matt scrambled onto the grass and immediately ran to the back of the bug. He looked up and down the rows of scrap airbugs. There was no sign of Targon. The back of his neck went hot and then cold. What had become of his friend?

He heard a sound behind him. Matt turned to see Targon crawl out from the cockpit of the bug next to them.

"Whew! That was close!" Targon smiled. "Angel, I

found another plate. Got the tools so we can get it?"

Matt's bottom jaw dropped. "Zang it! You were there
. . . in the bug next to us . . . the whole time?"

Targon nodded. "Yeah. I was nearly back here when
the Vorgs arrived. You know, you don't look very well,
Matt."

Matt sighed. "That's because I was worried about
you! I was afraid you hadn't heard the Vorg patrol in
time."

Targon grinned. "Nice of you to worry—but no one
could have missed *that* noise. I know the sound of an
airbug by now!"

Matt sat on the grass and waited for Angel and
Targon to return with the registration plate. He couldn't
believe that Targon wasn't more shaken by the
experience. At least they were all okay . . . all except for
Varl. What had become of his elderly friend? Matt knew
he must retrieve his computer. Then they could work out
where to look for him.

"This is perfect," said Angel, returning with Targon.
She showed Matt their find.

"Shall we put our plate on the blue bug?" asked
Targon.

Angel shook her head as she set to work. "No, we'll
take it with us. Otherwise, if the Vorgs search the
graveyard and recognize the numbers, they'll know what
we've done. Okay, let's get this in place."

"794283," said Targon, as she put in the final pin.
"That's a lucky number."

"It is?" asked Angel.

"Joke!" said Targon, breaking into fits of laughter.

Angel laughed too. "Okay, you got me—this time."

Matt jumped into the front middle seat. Targon and Angel clambered in on either side.

"Right, let's get out of here," said Matt.

"North or South?" asked Angel.

"How about searching for an old barn?" suggested Matt, looking at Targon with pursed lips.

Angel raised her eyebrows. "You're kidding, right? I said you wouldn't catch me off-guard a second time."

"It's no joke," said Matt. "We have something very important to find that we hid from the Vorgs. We hope you'll help us."

Angel fiddled with her earrings. She looked at him suspiciously. "What exactly do you need to find?"

"Matt's computer," said Targon.

"A computer?"

"It has the latest upgrades and a lot of technical programs on it," said Matt, thinking quickly. "It could help the Resistance defeat the Vorgs."

Targon looked at Matt with a mystified expression.

"Hmm," said Angel. "I know the Resistance couldn't get Govan equipment out of Bay City in time. They had to destroy a lot of our software before the Vorgs got hold of it, and what was left, the Vorgs destroyed anyway. I suppose a computer could be very useful."

"Then we'll join the Resistance," added Matt. He hoped she wouldn't be able to refuse his offer. "That's what you think we should do, isn't it?"

Angel nodded. "If we can find them."

"How about it, Angel?" Matt pushed.

"Okay, where's this barn?"

Matt bit his lip. "We're not exactly sure. There's an animal trough outside."

"And . . . it's roughly where?"

Matt shrugged.

Angel grimaced. "Do you know how many *thousands* of barns and animal troughs there are around here? You can't honestly expect us to find one of them from that tiny piece of non-technical data you've just given me! You've got to be mad! An animal trough?"

"I think we can narrow it down a little," said Targon.

Matt looked at him hopefully. What extra information did Targon have, exactly?

"I'm a good judge of time. I have to be. I can't read a clock, you see." Targon looked embarrassed. "It took us no more than ten minutes by airbug from the barn to Bay City."

Angel screamed between her teeth. "But that still could be anywhere! We need a direction. *Do* you know the approximate direction?"

Matt thought out loud. "We were walking north toward the city."

"And you know this because . . .?" asked Angel skeptically.

"Because the sun sets in the west and we watched it go down on our left hand side as we walked. That means we were coming from the south and heading north."

Angel sighed. "That's a start. Not really much to go on, though."

"How about we use the airbug computer? We approximate the average speed of an airbug. Then we use a ten-minute radius at that speed to plot a circle around Bay City. Along that radius, to the south of the city, is where we search," suggested Matt.

"Sounds like a plan to me," said Targon, fastening his seat belt.

Angel fired up the engines. "I think it's an impossible task. But, if we can help the Resistance, I'll go along with it . . . for now."

Matt felt guilty as they lifted off. When telling Angel about his computer he had exaggerated its usefulness to the Resistance. He had a feeling that when she saw his laptop from 2010 she'd wonder where he'd got such an outdated piece of equipment. How would he convince her that it was of value? Would she go along with him and Targon a second time?

Chapter 9

M att grew more depressed as the afternoon sun began to fade. Angel had been at the wheel for nearly three hours and they had visited over a dozen barns without success. Targon had been right. One barn looked like another, and they all looked different in daylight. On a positive note, only one airbug had been sighted. Angel had taken evasive action and quickly set them down close to a clump of tall pine trees. She was becoming familiar with the controls and landed the craft with ease.

Matt was also more confident with the airbug computer system. He opened up the landscape profile on the computer for the hundredth time. He sighed as he began searching the list of documented buildings again.

"There has to be a way to narrow down our choices," said Matt. "Isn't there anything else we saw or passed?"

"Farm tracks," suggested Targon. "We were on a farm track not long before we turned onto the main road and walked by the barn."

Matt smiled. "That might do it!" He keyed *'search farm tracks'* into the computer and looked to see where they were marked in relation to the barns. He immediately ruled out several they had already visited and another three that were too far south, according to

Targon's time calculation.

"Great going, Targon! That narrows it right down. There are only four more possibilities in this area," he said, rubbing his forehead. "After that, we'd better try farther south."

"It'll be dark in an hour," said Angel. "We'll have to start looking for somewhere to hide the airbug for the night."

"There's one, down there!" said Targon, pointing to another barn. "Try that one."

Angel swooped low. There was an animal trough to the side of the barn doors.

"Let's land," said Matt, scouring the skies. "I don't see any Vorgs. We'll risk it."

Angel slowed the engines and turned on the air cushion. They hovered for a few seconds and gently put down.

Matt scrambled over Targon and ran to the trough. Excitedly, he felt inside the gap. He ran his hands from one side to the other. He couldn't feel his computer. He pushed his hand lower until his upper arm became wedged. Where was it? His excitement turned to despair. The computer wasn't there.

Targon ambled up behind. "This barn's too new," he groaned. "*Our* barn was so old the wood was rotten. This one's been freshly painted."

Matt stood up and studied the barn doors in the evening haze. Targon was right. The wood on *their* barn was so rotten the doors wouldn't budge. On this one the hinges had even been replaced.

Matt kicked the dirt in frustration. "I'm beginning to think it's a lost cause."

Targon slapped him on the back. "Let's not give up yet," he whispered. "If Varl were here, he'd continue."

"We don't have a choice," said Matt. "We *have* to find my computer—unless you want to stay here. How much longer can we persuade Angel to keep looking?"

Matt and Targon climbed back into the cockpit.

"The light's fading fast," moaned Angel. "I've got to put the bug's lights on and I'm tired. We'll have to find somewhere for the night and make new plans. We've already risked being caught by landing here."

"One last try," begged Matt. "There's another barn really close."

"I'll make you a deal," said Angel in a craggy tone. "One more barn, but if that isn't it, we quit."

" . . . for the night," added Matt, hopeful that he'd be able to convince her to continue in the morning.

Angel frowned but said nothing. She pulled the airbug up again. Matt gave her new coordinates. They headed over fields of corn with scraggy oaks dotting the landscape. Matt looked down at the road below. In the low light, he could just make out deep crevices in the surface. It seemed familiar.

Matt felt a tingling sensation in his hands. His pulse quickened. "This is it," he said with confidence.

"You sure?" asked Angel, her tone carrying a hint of irritation.

"He's right," agreed Targon. "There's the ditch running alongside the field."

"And I remember seeing that white house in the distance." added Matt.

"I don't see a barn," said Angel. She shook her head and sighed.

"Turn around," demanded Matt. "Follow the road south, away from Bay City."

Angel maneuvered the craft easily. She turned and dipped lower.

"There!" screamed Matt. The airbug's lights illuminated the outline of a barn. "That's it. I can see the trough from here." He clapped his hands together in excitement. "I knew it!"

"Okay, we'll put down," groaned Angel, "or you'll never let me hear the end of it." She cut the engine speed and began the descent. "Vorgs!" she screamed. "I saw flashes of light through the clouds."

"Where?" asked Matt. He looked frantically through the windshield.

"They're above."

"Did they see us?"

"Don't know," replied Angel. She chewed her bottom lip. "There's more than one airbug. What shall we do?"

"When the cloud cover goes, we'll be an easy target," said Targon.

"Turn out the bug's lights, and put us down on the far side of the barn," instructed Matt.

"Are you mad? If they see us on the ground, we're

done for. It'll take too long to lift off again," Angel argued.

"I've got to get my computer!" said Matt, slamming his hand down on the console. "I'm not leaving it a second time. Besides, we can't fly low without lights—we'll hit the trees, and we don't want to be up at their height."

"He's right," agreed Targon. "It's the most sensible thing to do."

Angel gritted her teeth and growled in protest. She turned off the lights and lowered the bug behind the barn.

Matt jumped out and ran around the corner to the animal trough. His heart skipped a beat as he shoved his hand into the crack. *Please let it still be there*, he said to himself. He felt a smooth surface and then the raised edges of a hinge.

"Yes!" he cheered, as he pushed his laptop along to the end of the crack with his fingertips.

When the computer protruded several inches from behind the trough, Matt took hold of the end of his prized possession and tugged it free. He ran back to the bug with a huge smile across his face. He was ecstatic. Now he could begin Level 3 of his game and find Varl.

Targon and Angel were waiting anxiously.

"Did you get it?" asked Targon, moving into the center seat.

"Got it," he responded, scrambling in.

Targon looked at the familiar cracked lid. "Zang it! That's the best news we've had in a long time!"

Angel said nothing about the computer. Matt could

see that her eyes were focused on the darkening sky above.

"I can still see lights," she said. "I think the Vorgs are circling. They probably caught a glimpse of our lights."

Matt squinted in the near darkness. "Are there doors on this side of the barn as well?"

"Looks like it," replied Targon.

Matt leaned across Targon to talk to Angel. "Do you think we could get the airbug into the barn?"

"What do you mean?"

"The front doors are too rotten to budge. If we can open the barn's side doors, do you think you could maneuver the bug inside?"

"Possibly," said Angel. "The barn's tall enough. It might be tight on the width, but we could try."

"Let's go, Targon," said Matt, urging his friend to get out and help.

Matt ran to the doors. It was difficult to see without the bug's lights. He felt for the handles and tugged. The doors moved slightly but seemed to be fastened.

"Do you feel a bolt?" he asked Targon.

Targon felt along the bottom edge of the doors. "There's one here," he said, easing it from side to side. "Got it! Now try."

Matt tugged again. The doors rattled and showed some movement, but were still latched somehow. "There must be another." The cloud cover broke for just a few seconds and light from the moon glinted off metal on the door. "I think I saw a latch in the middle."

"It's just out of reach," groaned Targon, jumping up in an effort to knock it free. "Another year of growing and I'd have got it easily."

Angel was agitated. "Forget it, Matt. It's best we get out of here, while we've got the chance."

Matt ignored her. He knew that this was a good idea. If they could shelter in the barn for the night, they would be out of view of the Vorgs and could rest easy.

"I'll lift you up there, Targon." He stooped low and Targon clambered onto his shoulders. Matt stood up and staggered a few paces as he regained his balance. "Can you reach it now?"

"No problem," said Targon. He grunted and groaned as he shoved at the metal latch. "It won't budge."

Matt held Targon's legs tightly. "It may have rusted," he panted. "Go on—give it some effort!"

"Got it!" said Targon, toppling from Matt's shoulders with the force of the final shove. He stumbled as he landed.

"Okay, we'll take a door each," said Matt, grabbing a handle.

"Hurry," Angel shouted. "The moon is about to break through the clouds again. If the Vorgs come any lower, they'll see us."

The huge barn doors grated along the ground. Matt tugged and pulled. He dug his heels in the dirt and used every bit of strength he could muster. Slowly, the gap widened and the door swung back flat against the side of the barn. Matt ran over to Targon's side and yanked with him on the other door. It was stuck. They paused to get their breath.

"Once more," gasped Matt.

They pulled together. The concerted effort finally paid off, and the second door swung back against the barn.

Angel wasted no time. She fired up the airbug and maneuvered into position. "How am I doing?"

"You're okay on this side," said Matt, giving her a thumbs up.

"There's a hand width to spare over here," shouted Targon.

Matt looked at the height. There was plenty of room. He beckoned to her to continue. Angel inched through the opening until the front of the air cushion touched the barn wall on the other side. Angel cut the engines and raised the back door of the bug.

Matt and Targon pulled the huge barn doors closed. The barn was now pitch black inside. Matt felt his way over to the airbug.

"I'll put one of the small emergency floor lights on," called Angel. "We can't risk turning on the main lights. There are cracks in the wooden slats and it's dark outside. We'll be seen."

Suddenly, a faint glimmer of yellow light illuminated his path. Matt grabbed his computer from the cockpit and clambered into the back of the bug alongside Angel. She sat on the padded seats, head in hands.

"That wasn't so difficult, was it?" said Matt, placing

his computer on his lap.

She let out an enormous sigh. "I guess it was worth being able to sleep in safety tonight."

Targon stretched out on the bench opposite where Matt and Angel sat. "You're so right!" He yawned and rolled over on his side. "I feel like I haven't slept in weeks. Wake me in a few hours."

Matt opened his laptop. He turned on the power and waited anxiously for the game to load. Angel leaned toward him and stared at the computer. Matt could see the bemused expression on her face in the yellow glow.

"I thought you said your computer had the latest upgrades. This one looks like something my great-grandpa would have used!" she smirked. "Where'd you get it—the junkyard?"

Matt tilted the screen away from her view and watched his *Keeper of the Kingdom* game load as she talked. He pressed *'Level 3'*, pulled up the *'Menu'*, and selected *'Rules.'* "My dad got it for me. It's the latest Pentium model."

"*Pentium*? They went out with the automobile!" Angel laughed. "My computer's a Xandix III."

"Oh, really. *Only* a Xandix. Not that great, then," replied Matt, not knowing what to say. *Xandix III*? *What was that*?

Angel frowned. "You're really something, Matt Hammond. I can't figure you out. Just when I think you're joking or you're a complete idiot, you surprise me. What's it to be this time?"

Matt grinned. "I'm about to surprise you again. This is the Pentium . . . um . . . XIR3205—it only came out at the beginning of the year.   Wait 'til you see what it can do. This program will tell us how to find the Resistance," he said with confidence.

She rolled her eyes and taunted him. "And how's it going to do that? No one knows where the Resistance has set up base. You don't go to them—they come to you."

"Watch," he said, turning the screen toward her. Matt scrolled down the list of options. "What did I tell you? *'Number 3, The Resistance'.*"

"This I've got to see," Angel snorted. She slapped Matt's hand out of the way of the keyboard and pressed *'Enter'* before he could object.   "Let's see what this supposed state-of-the-art machine is capable of."

Matt held his breath. Would she be fooled?

An idyllic seascape filled the screen. To the sound of peaceful violin music, waves crashed on the shore. Tall cliffs dominated the background. Gulls circled in the clear blue sky, swooping down to the water for fish.

Angel's eyes grew wide. "That's part of the coastal walk in Bay City Nature Preserve."

"You sure?" asked Matt.

She gave Matt a broad smile. "No question. I've been there loads of times."

"There'll be a riddle," said Matt as words began to replace the picture. "If we can solve it, we'll find the Resistance."

"A riddle? What kind of program is this? Sounds more like a game."

Matt's heart raced. *A game? She was too smart.* He felt sure that she could see his red face even in the low light of the computer screen. He covered his face with his hands as if he were thinking. "The program is really clever. It tests your ingenuity," he said quickly. "You have to show you are worthy of receiving the information."

Angel pulled a disbelieving grimace. She shook her head, her ginger curls bouncing from side to side. "Pentium XIR3205, eh? Sounds too much like hard work to me. Computers are supposed to make life easier!"

"You don't get anything for nothing in this world. It teaches you that," said Matt, repeating something Mrs. Tanyard had said during one of his English lessons. "Here's the rhyme. What do you make of it?"

In Level 3 rules will change
Activate the Keeper to win the game
Use the Resistance and their might
To destroy the Vorgs in dead of night
In the cliffs of Gova's coast
Locate the network of your host
Learn about those who invade
Their Achilles' heel is your crusade

"Targon, what do you think?" asked Matt.
Matt looked up from his laptop when there was no

reply. Targon was in a deep sleep.

Angel played with her gold earrings while staring at the screen. "It seems to be telling us to search the Bay City Cliffs for the Resistance and to learn all about the Vorgs."

"I'd say that much is pretty obvious. Not quite sure I get the bit about Achilles' heel," said Matt, closing the program. "I think Achilles was an ancient Greek."

"That's all I know about him too." Angel yawned. "We'd better get out of here just after dawn. We'll see daylight through the cracks in the wood."

Matt closed his eyes. His spirits had lifted now that he had his computer back. Who was Achilles? What relevance was he to the Vorgs? He hoped that when they found the Resistance tomorrow, those questions would be answered. *If* they found the Resistance.

Chapter 10

Varl looked around the computer room. It was his second morning in the cliff homes with the Resistance. He felt depressed. Chip had warned him that not much equipment had been saved, but Varl hadn't been prepared for what he now saw. A mound of broken but salvageable computers occupied one corner, and wire and cables were coiled in another. Stacked along the length of an entire wall were large boxes labeled, 'components.' Only four computers, positioned on a bench just inside the door, seemed to be working. Varl opened one of the boxes and fingered some of the computer parts. Most were unfamiliar to him.

Chip gave him a sad grin. "This is all we managed to rescue."

"It's a start," said Varl, trying to raise his new friend's spirits. He walked over to a huge screen propped against some of the boxes. It was at least six feet square and less than an inch thick. "Never seen a monitor this size."

"It belongs to the new Xandix III," replied Chip. "These other functional computers are decades old." He pointed to a cube one-quarter the size of Matt's laptop. "We've been trying to rebuild the Xandix. We're nearly done."

Varl fingered the cube. "Tiny," he muttered. "What's

its capability?"

Chip chuckled. "It's so fast that information is brought up instantly."

"Is that so unusual?"

Chip smiled knowingly. "Its capabilities go well beyond that."

"How so?" asked Varl.

Chip picked up a helmet lying on the table next to the screen. "Once this is connected, the Xandix can read your mind and translate your thoughts into documents instantly. If you have questions, the answers will be on the screen before you've even finished the thought."

"Impressive," said Varl, turning the helmet in his hands.

"*And*," continued Chip, "I've saved the best for last."

Varl raised his eyebrows. "I can hardly wait," he laughed.

"We've created an elaborate Xandix III network. It was developed as a security system for Bay City residents. The Vorgs are unaware, but every government and public building in Bay City had Xandix technology installed before their arrival. Some residents of Bay City protested, saying that it was like being spied upon everywhere they went. But in the end, many private companies and homes also had the system installed. Once this baby is linked into the network we'll be able to see into just about any building now occupied by Vorgs, without them knowing."

Varl hesitated. He didn't want to dash Chip's hopes,

but he had to ask the ultimate question. "Surely the Vorgs will have found the cameras and network transmitters and destroyed them all by now."

"Cameras?" Chip laughed. "You're way behind the times. We use optics, which are microscopic wireless transmitters no bigger than a freckle on your hand. There are up to one hundred in any one room, giving a complete 360-degree view. Each optic sends its signals to a trimod." Chip walked over to one of the boxes of components and rummaged in the top. He pulled out a small silver pyramid no bigger than his thumb, and turned it lovingly in the palm of his hand. "One of these tiny trimods is hidden in the walls of every room of every government building in Bay City. Each trimod is a computer and receiver linked to the Xandix network."

Varl felt awkward asking so many questions but he needed to know the complete situation. "Isn't it possible that the Vorgs learned about the network from the computer files left in Bay City?"

"Within hours of their arrival, the Vorgs smashed their way through every building in Bay City. They destroyed all communication modes, including computer terminals and even time machines, to stop humans from communicating. This allowed the Vorgs to gain control quickly, and it denied us the chance to regroup and defend ourselves."

"Makes good strategic sense," muttered Varl.

Chip was positively beaming as he continued with the tale. "*But*, by doing so, the Vorgs made a huge blunder.

They failed to evaluate our technical abilities and have no knowledge of the network. The structure of the Xandix system is still safely buried in the walls."

Varl raised his eyebrows. "But how can you tap into the network from here and receive signals? Wireless transmitters are useless through rock walls. The walls of these caves must be several feet thick."

"Correct. The system was set up so that cables could be used as an emergency backup. We have electricity in the cave complex, as you are aware. Snake has already run network cables through the sewer system to connect us with one of the three hidden receiver stations we built on the outskirts of the city." Chip held up the trimod above his head. "As long as these beauties are not discovered, and the Vorgs remain focused on their own plans, we'll be connected back into the network in a couple of days. The only building we won't be able to infiltrate is the Great Complex."

"Why is that?" asked Varl.

"The Vorgs built it when they arrived as their center of operations. We'd have to get someone inside the building to install the trimods and optics. It's a long job, and not one that someone can do without being seen. It would be a death sentence for anyone attempting it, and could cost us the network if we're discovered."

"Hmm," grunted Varl. "On the other hand, we'd get a better idea of what we're up against if we could witness the Vorgs' technology firsthand and hear their plans for Bay City."

"Agreed," said Chip.

"I'll think about that one," said Varl,

Snake entered the room, gasping for breath. "Bad news, mates. An airbug's been spotted circling the cliffs."

"We're coming," replied Chip, almost dropping the trimod. He turned to Varl. "Sorry, but our conversation will have to continue at another time. I need to help the others evaluate if we're in any kind of danger."

Varl quickly put down the helmet. "I'm coming too."

* * * * *

Angel swooped the airbug low over the cliffs in the early morning sun.

"Here we go for the fourth time," said Matt, frustrated. Why couldn't something be easy for once? "This is as difficult as trying to find my computer yesterday."

"See anything?" she asked.

Matt shook his head. "We're not really close enough. I think I'd be able to spot movement but that's about all. From this height there could be a Vorg *or* a human on the ground—it would be hard to tell."

Angel sighed. "Trouble is, the Resistance will see the airbug and assume *we're* Vorgs. They'll stay hidden."

"You're right," said Matt. "Perhaps we'll have to take the risk and land on the cliff top. If we hike along the footpath we might be rescued by someone."

"I'll head back out to sea and circle one last time," said Angel with resignation.

"Pity we can't signal or something," muttered Targon.

"That's it! You've done it again!" cheered Matt.

"I have?" asked Targon, with a baffled look on his face. "How?"

Matt could hardly contain his excitement. He turned to Angel. "There are lights on this thing, right?"

Angel nodded. "You know there are. How's that going to help? Flashing the airbug lights won't tell the Resistance who we are."

Matt smiled at her. "It will if someone on the ground can read a coded message."

"But how do you know that someone else will be able to read *your* code?" asked Targon.

"My dad taught me Morse code for a school science fair project. It was a communication system developed by a man called Samuel Morse in the 1840s. The code consisted of short and long electrical signals, which were sent down wires."

"The 1840s?" spluttered Targon. "That's ancient! It's now 2540, so that's . . ."

"Around 700 years ago," laughed Angel. "I learned about Morse Code in school. It's a good system when you're almost without technology, but what are the chances of someone else knowing it in this day and age? You don't think your dad found the Resistance and is down there too, do you?"

Matt grinned. He couldn't exactly tell Angel that his dad was waiting for him to return 500 years in the past. "My dad's . . . umm . . ." stammered Matt.

"Oh, I'm sorry," replied Angel, obviously assuming the worst. Her face took on a grim expression. She stared ahead out the window and mumbled, "The Vorgs have destroyed a lot of families."

Matt touched her hand gently. "It's worth a try, isn't it?"

"But we don't have wires to send messages down," argued Targon.

"No, but I can flash the airbug lights as short or long signals instead," said Matt excitedly. "Sailors used to do it in emergencies. That's how the SOS system was started."

"SOS?" repeated Targon.

"Save our souls," said Matt. "In the old days, if a ship was in trouble, that's the message they'd send by flashing huge lights on the boat's deck."

"Do you know the whole alphabet?" asked Angel.

Matt shook his head. "I can spell out SOS, my full name—Matthew Reagan Hammond—and the word 'help'."

"*Three* names?" said Targon. "I've only got the one."

"Hammond is my family name and my mom chose Reagan to make my grandpa happy. He admired the 40th president of the United States."

"The who?" said Targon.

Angel laughed. "What good is knowing your full name in Morse code? Who in the Resistance is likely to know who *you* are?"

Matt shrugged. "No one. But Matthew Reagan

Hammond has exactly eleven different letters in it. The word 'help' has another two different letters, and then there's the 'S' in SOS. There must be something we can spell out with fourteen letters."

"Targon's name, for starters," said Angel.

Targon grinned. "*I* knew that," he said quickly.

Matt smiled at his friend. He guessed that Targon didn't want Angel to know that he couldn't read or write.

"And mine, actually," said Angel with a surprised look on her face. "Amazing what you can spell with fourteen letters. Okay, it's worth a try."

She slowed the engine speed, turned the airbug around over the open water and headed back toward the cliffs.

Matt hurriedly brought up the program controls and began accessing data on the airbug lights. "I might even be able to program a flashing sequence into this thing," he muttered. "Then we could get it to repeat the same pattern over and over again."

"What words do you have in mind?" asked Targon.

"Our three names, followed by the words, 'WE ARE NOT VORGS.'"

"Impressive," said Angel. "Just one problem."

"Which is?" asked Matt, still selecting options from the screen.

"You don't know how to do the letter V so you can only spell ORGS."

Matt clenched his teeth. "Oh, yeah. Zang it! It was a good idea, too." Angel was a quick thinker and a better speller.

"You should still try it," said Targon, pushing Matt toward the screen again. "Anyone who could read the code might get the message. They'd just think you didn't work it out correctly."

Matt sighed. "Could be. It's a long shot, but I guess it's still worth a try."

"Anything's worth a try," said Targon. "The last thing I want is to be caught by the Vorgs again."

Matt set to work. He felt fairly confident about programming the airbug computer, but he was definitely rusty on the Morse code. "Okay, I've managed to access the lights data. Now I'll enter a sequence of long and short flashes," he replied. "Let's hope I can remember the code for each letter."

Angel nudged Matt. "You'll have to do this quickly. We'll be approaching the cliffs in five minutes at our current speed. If this doesn't work, we'll have to land and take our chances on foot."

* * * * *

Varl followed Chip and Snake to the entrance of the cave dwelling. The enormous opening appeared to be a wall of solid rock. Bee was standing with Fly, staring at a screen mounted on the wall.

"What do you make of it?" Varl asked.

"It's strange," replied Bee, without turning to look at him. "The airbug is circling in a way I've not seen before.

The Vorgs normally fly along the coast checking the cliff-top path for runaway humans. This is the fifth time this bug has approached us from the sea and headed straight for the cliffs. It's almost as if they know about the entrance."

"But they can't see it, right?" asked Varl.

"Correct," answered Chip. "The simulated wall is still up. We managed to salvage outdated cameras and install them along the beach, path and cliff face. They allow us to see what is going on directly outside. All Resistance members have a small device that lowers the entrance wall as they approach by jetpack."

"Can you get a closer look at the airbug?" asked Varl.

Chip shook his head. "We're at full camera range now."

"What's with the lights?" asked Snake.

"Lights?" questioned Bee and Chip in unison.

Varl stared at the screen with the others. Snake was right. It appeared that the airbug's lights were flashing.

"It's probably just the angle of the sun on the sea," said Bee. "The sun can play strange tricks on the eyes."

"Don't think so," muttered Varl.

"What are you seeing?" asked Chip.

Varl stroked his chin and frowned. "There seems to be a pattern."

"What do you mean, mate?" asked Snake.

"I can see it now," agreed Fly. "Some light flashes are short and some are long. Watch. First there's two long flashes then a break, then a short and a long and another break, then a long and a break, and another long and a break."

"What do you s'ppose it means?" asked Snake.

"I think it's Morse," said Varl. "Morse code was developed hundreds of years ago."

"I do believe you're right," said Chip. "I've seen it done before, but never with lights."

"The airbug's reduced its speed. It's approaching the beach. Could be a trap," said Bee without hesitation. "The Vorgs can be very cunning."

"Anyone got a pen?" asked Varl.

"A pen? They became obsolete decades ago!" Chip dug into his pants and produced a small flat instrument that fit snugly into the palm of his hand. "No pen, but I do have a micruter."

"Micruter?" questioned Varl.

"It's a tiny computer. Read out the sequence and I'll enter it."

Varl concentrated hard on the flashing lights. "o-r-g-s," he said out loud.

"Orgs? What's that, do you think?" asked Chip.

"Perhaps you missed the first letter and it is supposed to be the word Vorgs," said Bee.

"Vorgs?" said Snake. "That's it . . . I'm out of 'ere!"

"Wait—not so fast," snapped Varl. "There's more. The lights are starting again. Take this down, Chip. I'll dictate each letter. M-A-T-T . . . T-A-R-G-O-N . . . A-N-G-E-L . . . W-E . . . A-R-E . . . N-O-T . . . O-R-G-S. It's my friends!" said Varl, choking on the words.

"What do you mean?" asked Chip, reading back the letters.

Varl laughed. "Open the door, now! Let the airbug in! It's Matt and Targon—the boys that I told you about. Those kids never cease to amaze me!"

"Could be a trap," said Bee, grabbing Chip's arm before he could press the door remote. "The Vorgs are cunning. Perhaps they caught and interrogated your young friends, Varl."

Varl shook his head. "Matt's a smart one. I doubt if the Vorgs would know Morse code, but Matt might. Open the door, *please*."

Chip seemed to be hesitating, his hand suspended over the remote control. Varl knew he couldn't explain that Matt was from 500 years in Chip's past and therefore could easily have read about and learned Morse code.

"What about Angel?" questioned Bee. "Who is that?"

"Look, I have no idea," snapped Varl, anxious that the boys might fly off without knowing he was here. "Why would the Vorgs send one airbug to fly blindly into a Resistance camp?"

"It may just be a ploy to get us to reveal our location," reasoned Chip. "The bug could turn around, once it has marked our hideout, and return with reinforcements."

Varl sighed. They were right of course, and he couldn't blame them for being cautious. How could he convince Chip and Bee otherwise? "Let's send a message back," shouted Varl. "Quick! Before they give up and go away. Use the outside light on the cliff path."

"Seems a reasonable idea," said Chip. "What do you want to say?"

"Ask them the question, *Who is the old man from Zaul?*"

Chip looked puzzled, but flashed the light control as Varl gave him the sequence. They waited for the response, eyes glued to the screen. They waited . . . and waited . . . and waited. The airbug was now hovering directly outside.

Chip tapped his foot rhythmically on the floor. "Seems Bee was right," he said impatiently.

"I don't like this," snapped Bee. "What onboard weapons does an airbug carry? Could they blast their way through the cliff face?"Chip put his hand on her shoulder. "Don't worry—it's a civilian bug—not military." "Give them time," replied Varl, hopefully. He looked at his watch. "Only two minutes have passed."

The airbug lights began to flash.

"There!" said Varl, grinning excitedly as the reply came back.

"What's it say?" demanded Snake.

"A-R-L. They're spelling my name."

"Not exactly," said Bee. "What about the V?"

Varl laughed. "Don't you see? Matt couldn't spell Vorg either—he's forgotten the code for the letter V."

Chip chuckled. "Okay, that's good enough for me."

Bee shook her head. "I'm not convinced, but I'm willing to take the risk as long as this whole facility is put on red alert."

"Snake, pass the word around that we're expecting visitors," instructed Chip. "Do it quickly. Tell everyone Code Red."

"Okay, raise the door," said Bee, "but be prepared to close it fast if anything seems amiss as they approach."

Varl watched the huge opening appear in the rock face. He had felt so certain that his friends had sent the message a few minutes before. Now he wondered if he had placed everyone's life at risk in his eagerness to see Matt and Targon again. It was too late to change his mind. He watched the approaching airbug with apprehension.

Chapter 11

Jesper of the Mount stood on the cliff overlooking the bay. His purple cloak flapped in the strong sea breeze. He peeked at the crashing waves below, dizzy with the height. Perhaps he should jump and be done with it. Better that than bring shame on his family. He hung his head. For one so brave and fearless, one who had led Vorgs across the galaxy and conquered many planets, he was suddenly too cowardly to take his own life. No, he would be more courageous to face up to the situation and do something about it. He took a step back from the edge.

"You'll be sorry, Gubala," he hissed. "The humans will soon see what fools you all are. So many battles have been lost over the centuries by Vorg leaders too arrogant and confident to see the enemy's strengths." He felt certain that Gubala was about to make the same mistake. "Humans may not be able to match our might, but many of them are cunning and intelligent. I will wait patiently for your downfall."

A flash of light caught his attention. Jesper focused on the cloudless sky. Could it be? Yes . . . it was an airbug. What was it doing flying in from the sea? Normal Vorg patrol routes followed along the cliffs.

Jesper hid behind a cluster of boulders and watched the airbug approach. Its gleaming silver body seemed to be catching the sun, or was it flashing its lights? Was it in distress? He expected the bug would attempt an emergency landing. Instead it approached the cliff face, barely within his vision. Then suddenly it disappeared. He waited for the sound of a crashing vehicle, but all he heard were the waves pounding on the shore.

Jesper sprang from his hiding place, thrusting his tongue over the edge of his jaw. Where had it gone? He ventured near the cliff edge and held his breath as he peered below, half expecting to see pieces of wreckage strewn on the rocks. There were none. He looked at the tall red-brown cliffs, wondering if the sun had played tricks on his sight. Unable to answer any of his own questions, he grunted in disbelief and headed back along the grassy path to Bay City. Yesterday's events had turned his life upside down. Now he was losing his mind, as well as his job.

* * * * *

Matt stared ahead at the wall of rock. The airbug was closing in fast. "It's no good. Pull the airbug up, Angel! We'll have to turn and make one last attempt."

An enormous cavern suddenly appeared in the cliff face.

"What the . . .?" he said, mouth gaping.

Targon was speechless, his eyes wide.

"I guess we've found the Resistance," said Angel with a broad smile. She maneuvered the airbug into position in front of the opening.

"You don't seem surprised at all!" exclaimed Targon. "How did this hole appear from nowhere?"

Angel tossed back her thick hair and laughed loudly. "A lot of people told me there was no such thing as the Resistance—they said it was just a story to keep everyone's hopes alive. But I never gave up looking. I *knew* they were real, and I knew they'd have a great hiding place."

She hesitated at the entrance and hovered for a few seconds. There was little room to spare on either side of the airbug.

"Easy does it," said Matt as she guided the craft carefully into the cavern. He exhaled when Angel cut the power and the bug came to rest softly on the rocky floor. "You're getting good at this," he complimented her.

Matt looked through the cockpit window. He swallowed hard. Many weapons were aimed at them. This was not the reception he had anticipated.

"Get out of the airbug . . . and no fast moves," ordered a deep voice.

Angel raised her hands in the air, a look of bewilderment on her face. She slid slowly from the cockpit seat. Matt followed her. His hands shook as he stepped out and walked in front of the airbug to stand next to Angel. Targon exited from the other side and joined them.

"Lower your weapons. These are my friends," Varl bellowed. He pushed through the crowd that had gathered at the entrance.

Matt shrieked with delight. "Varl! I knew it!"

"Who else would be able to read something as ancient as Morse code?" said Targon, wrapping his arms around Varl's waist.

"Me, actually," said Chip, stepping forward. He shook Matt's hand first and then Targon's. "I'm Chip. Pleased to meet you. You're a clever bunch of kids. I'm impressed with your knowledge and ingenuity." He turned to Angel. "As for you, young lady, your flying skills are impressive!"

Angel blushed. "Thanks," she replied. "I hope the Resistance can use an airbug!"

Chip smoothed his hand over his bald head and chuckled. "I would say we have just acquired an important asset in our campaign against the Vorgs." He studied the bug carefully, with a wide grin fixed on his face.

"Angel . . . Angel. Is that you?" questioned a voice in the crowd.

"Who's asking?" said Angel, twisting around and scouring the sea of faces.

Matt turned to see a hand wave madly above the sea of heads.

"It's me . . . Fly."

"Fly? Fly, is it really you?" Angel's expression was one of utter shock. She stepped forward and jumped up and down, obviously trying to see his face.

The crowd moved apart to let through a tall young man with a Mohawk haircut. Matt watched Angel melt. Tears ran down her cheeks. She threw her arms around Fly, almost strangling him. Whoever Fly was, he didn't seem to mind. Matt liked this softer side of Angel.

After a few seconds, Angel brushed away her tears and turned to face her friends. She gripped Fly's hand and looked radiant. "Matt, Targon, I'd like you to meet my big brother."

Matt smiled. He touched Angel on the arm and said, "That's really great, Angel. This must be the best present ever." It was a genuine expression of happiness for Angel after all that she had endured, but inside, Matt felt a pang of envy. He missed his own brother. Jake was great with computer games—if only he were here to help him play this one!

Matt tried not to let anyone see his sadness as he shook Fly's hand and met everyone else. How many days had he been gone on his adventures? He had lost count. Varl and Targon had become his family. Perhaps now that the three of them were together again, he could work out a way to win Level 3 of his game and get home to his real family. He grabbed his computer from inside the airbug and held it against his chest. One thing was sure—the Vorgs would not be easy to beat.

* * * * *

Jesper entered his old office in The Factory. He

collected his personal belongings off his desk and walked toward the door.

Harless of the Waters blocked his exit. His pale yellow eyes seemed to be laughing at Jesper.

"Couldn't stay away?" Harless sneered.

"Don't worry, I'm not here to contest your appointment as Commander of The Factory," said Jesper, unable to hide his sadness. "Just had to pick up a few personal things."

Harless tapped the acrylic photo frame in Jesper's claws. "You're too soft," he snorted. "Your mind's been elsewhere for days. You'd better get used to Earth. You've got another two years of this tour of duty—unless you fail at your next assignment too."

"Thank you for stating the obvious," said Jesper, pushing past him into the corridor. "I'm well aware of my situation." He shoved the photo of his young son in front of Harless' face. "Every day this memento reminds me of the reason I am here. In only six more years Galatin 4 will collide with Vorgus and destroy our world. I will sleep easily knowing that my son will have a new planet on which to live, and that I helped to find it. Are your reasons for being here so honorable, Harless?"

"They are no doubt the same as mine," said a voice from behind.

Jesper turned around to see Yorak of the Vale leaning against the opposite wall. He had a smug expression on his face.

"And what might they be?" asked Jesper.

"Power," replied Yorak, hissing the word with malice. The tips of his two pointed front teeth showed menacingly between his jaws. "No one respects a weak Vorg. With strength comes power."

"And a fat paycheck!" added Harless. The ripples of leathery skin under his chin wobbled as he laughed.

"Which do you think your son will remember most as he grows old in the new world?" asked Yorak. "That his father was one of thousands who colonized the new planet, or that his father was a great Vorg commander?"

"I know what my son will remember about me," hissed Harless. "The human holding cells are overcrowded. Now that *I'm* running The Factory, desensitization of humans will be increased to 750 a day and I'll clear the cells quickly. Gubala will be so pleased, he'll make me Supreme Commander. That's what *my* son will remember."

Jesper felt anger rise through his veins. It was all he could do to hold back his tongue from lashing out at Harless. "You wouldn't dare! Desensitization machines can operate for only two hours without a break, or they overheat and malfunction. To get that number of humans through the process in one day will require a shorter desensitization time and continuous operation of the equipment," he argued. "Without the necessary five minutes of desensitization and with malfunctioning machines, many humans will be permanently brain damaged or even killed."

"What do you care?" snarled Yorak. "We're here to

save Vorgs, not humans."

"Vorgs are *not* murderers!" retorted Jesper. "We are colonizing Earth because we have no choice, and we are desensitizing humans to make the takeover quick and easy, and to prevent bloodshed . . . but killing them? That was never part of the plan!"

"And you think that desensitization is better than death?" asked Yorak. His eyes narrowed. He pressed two claws into Jesper's chest and pushed him backward two steps. "You've been deluding yourself, Jesper. You have been inflicting a fate *worse* than death on humans. What Vorg would willingly go to The Gilded State? I'd rather die!"

Harless puffed out his chest. "The Great Gubala has instructed that we must get the Empire of Gova under our full control immediately. That means we must desensitize humans at a faster rate. The next craft from Vorgus is due to arrive with reinforcements in two days. We must be rid of the Govan Resistance and be ready to move inland to take the Colony of Javeer by then. I will do what is necessary to meet the deadline."

"May the great God have mercy on both your souls," said Jesper, walking away in disgust.

He turned the corner and slowed his pace, recalling their words. Venom rose in his mouth. A bitter taste sat on his tongue. They were right. He was no better than an executioner. Desensitization was painless but cruel. What Vorg would want to lose control of his thoughts? He had been justifying the process to himself all this time because humans did not die and Vorgs could conquer without bloodshed. But did that make it right?

"What has become of us?" he muttered. Vorgs had always respected every other life-form. Until the announcement of Galatin 4's collision course with Vorgus, Vorgs had not been interested in invading other planets. Now there was an urgency to find a new home—but was this the only way? He felt overwhelming sadness. What could he, one Vorg against so many, do to change the system?

Jesper passed by the materialization chamber and headed for the stairs. The way things had been going today, he didn't want to take his chances in the chamber. He climbed the steps to the airbug port on The Factory roof. Anger boiled in his gut. He felt anger at his harsh treatment by Gubala, anger at the conceit and blindness of his rivals, and anger at himself for what he had done to so many humans. He walked on to the flat roof and stepped into the brilliant sun.

"Wanting an airbug, sir?" asked Urg.

"Yes, thank you," replied Jesper.

"You'll have to wait around ten minutes, sir. We're short today. Still haven't recovered the bug that those young humans stole yesterday."

"Really?" said Jesper, recalling the airbug he had seen over the coast only three hours before. "Do you know what color it was?"

"Yes, I do, sir. I was part of the search party. It was silver, sir. The young pilot was a real hothead. She was hard to control when Renx and I captured her in a cornfield the day before. Determined little minx."

"You've been most helpful," said Jesper, his spirits lifting.

"Anytime, sir. There's a bug coming in now. You can sign it out." Urg handed him a pocket computer.

"Thank you, Urg." Jesper punched his code into the airbug log against the words: *registration no. 90423 - green.* He gave the device back. "How is Renx after yesterday's unfortunate accident?"

"He's in a lot of pain. He may be permanently blind, sir."

"I'm sorry to hear that. I hope that Harless will have the good sense to remove all of the canisters from The Factory walls so that there's no repeat of yesterday's attack."

"Sorry you won't be here at The Factory any longer, sir. I shouldn't say, but Harless of the Waters . . ."

Jesper nodded his head. "You needn't say any more. We understand each other. Thank you for your help and good wishes. There might come a time when I need to call on you for help."

"At your service, always, sir. I hope you know that there are many other Vorgs who would follow you."

Jesper lifted the end of his robe over his arm and climbed into the cockpit. He had always believed that most Vorgs liked and respected him as a leader. Urg had just confirmed that. It would be something to remember in the future.

For now he had to concentrate on finding the missing airbug and with it, he hoped, the Govan Resistance. He smiled with satisfaction. The day hadn't turned out so badly after all. He had work to do.

Chapter 12

"We'll put it in the corner," said Varl, positioning a mattress that Snake had just dragged through his bedroom door. "There . . . that'll do just fine."

Matt and Targon tested its softness. "Thanks, Snake," they said, almost in unison.

"Sorry we don't 'ave a spare room," Snake apologized. "B family's got crowded lately. Fly'll bring another mattress when 'e's finished givin' Angel a tour."

Matt smiled. "Don't worry. After a night in the back of an airbug and a night in The Factory, this will seem like heaven."

Snake's jaw dropped. "Really, mate? You've been inside The Factory?"

Targon groaned. "Not exactly a great experience or one I want to remember."

"You've been there, too? We thought only Varl 'ere had returned to tell what it's like inside!" said Snake, rubbing his hands together excitedly. "Chip will want to talk to you both right now. 'E's been trying to gather all the information 'e can about them Vorgs."

"I'll bring them along in about thirty minutes," said Varl, resting his hands on Snake's shoulders. "I need to spend a little time with my friends first."

Snake nodded. "Okay, mate. Understood."

Once Snake had left the room, Varl dug into his pocket and pressed the door control. He needed to talk to Matt and Targon without being overheard. As with the main entrance to the cliff homes, a solid wall suddenly formed in the opening.

"Well, we all made it," said Varl quietly. "And I even got some new clothes out of it. Like the color?" He modeled the bright red shirt that Spider had made, trying to joke a little and lighten the mood. After all, they were all together, which was something to celebrate. It just didn't feel like that since they had a lot of work to do to beat the Vorgs.

Matt ignored his comment. "How did you escape the Vorgs and desensitization?"

Varl gave up on his jovial mood. "It was close. I was lucky—especially since your *Keeper of the Kingdom* computer program dumped me in The Factory for the start of Level 3!"

"Seriously?" Matt shrieked. "I'm so sorry. At least Targon and I landed in a cornfield—even if there were Vorgs nearby."

Varl drew in a deep breath. He still found it hard to believe everything he had been through in the last two days. "I was disorientated. I had no idea who the Vorgs were or where I was. Suddenly a huge leathery-looking creature hauled me out from under a table. I'd never seen anything like it. I dived into a materialization chamber just as the doors were closing and escaped desensitization by a matter of minutes."

"That's some story," said Targon, hanging on every word. "And I thought *we* narrowly escaped."

"I'll tell you the rest later, and I want to hear your story too." Varl rubbed Matt's spiky hair affectionately. "I'm certainly very glad to see you both. I'd convinced myself that I was on my own this time."

Matt tapped his laptop. "I wouldn't leave you stranded," he laughed. "Besides, Varl, I don't think I can play the game without you. You seem to be a major player, and the Vorgs will be tough to beat."

"Ah, your computer game." Varl grinned knowingly.

"Still don't believe him?" asked Targon. "After everything we've been through, I sure do!"

Varl smiled. "Matt, my boy, everything you've ever said has turned out to be the truth, and every time we work out your game scenarios we seem to get out of the trouble we're in. I can't deny any of that. It's just a little hard for a scientist like me to believe I'm a character in a kid's computer game."

"I know," said Matt. "It's even hard for me to believe. I keep thinking I'm going to wake up from some terrible dream, but it never happens. Now the game scenario is coming together a *third* time."

"Fill me in," said Varl, getting comfortable on his bed.

"The first rhyme of Level 3 told us where to find the Resistance—and here we are," said Matt. "But there was a lot more information."

"Tell me what we've got to do," said Varl eagerly.

"The rhyme said we had to *activate* the Keeper to win

the game," Matt began.

"That's certainly different," said Varl, rubbing his chin. "In the first two levels the rhymes said to *destroy* the Keeper."

"What do you suppose the Keeper could be this time?" Targon interrupted.

Varl didn't need long to think about it. "*Activate* means to power up or start. That suggests the Keeper is either some type of computer or a piece of machinery."

"What about a bomb or other explosive device?" asked Matt.

"Or a vehicle?" added Targon.

"Could be," Varl agreed. "All of those ideas are possible. What else did the rhyme say?"

Matt opened his laptop and rested it on his legs. "It suggested using the Resistance to destroy the Vorgs in the dead of night."

"Hmm, a nighttime attack? That means flashlights and lack of sleep once again." Varl groaned and yawned at the thought.

"The last few lines gave us a clue about how to defeat the Vorgs that none of us understood," explained Matt.

"Go on," said Varl. "Tell me the lines."

"Here, you can read them," said Matt, pulling them up on the screen and handing the laptop to Varl.

Learn about those who invade
Their Achilles' heel is your crusade.

"Who or what was Achilles?" asked Matt. "Both Angel and I thought he was an ancient Greek."

"You were right," replied Varl. "Legend has it that Achilles was the mightiest of the Greeks who fought in the Trojan War. His mother, Thetis, had tried unsuccessfully to make him immortal. She held the young Achilles by the heel and dipped him in the river Styx. Everything the sacred waters touched became indestructible, but Achilles' heel remained dry and therefore unprotected. He was killed in battle when an arrow was shot into his heel."

"Zang it! What a story!" said Targon.

"Is someone's Achilles' heel the place where they are most vulnerable?" asked Matt.

"Exactly, my boy. The rhyme is telling us to look for the Vorgs' weakest spot as a way to defeat them."

"How do we do that?" asked Targon.

"We should be able to find out a lot more about the Vorgs once we get the Xandix III computer network fixed. Chip thinks he'll have the system running again in a day or two. "

"We just need to squirt them in the eyes with one of those silver canisters," said Targon, laughing. "That's their Achilles' heel. You should have seen that Vorg squeal and hiss yesterday!"

Matt stared, open-mouthed, at Targon. "Zang it, Targon—you keep getting these good ideas!"

"I do believe the boy's done it again," Varl said. He shook his head in disbelief. "For one who can't read or write, Targon, you certainly make up for it with your observations. Tell me more about this silver canister."

"I think it was a Govan fire extinguisher," said Matt. "They were hanging on the walls of The Factory."

"A purple mist filled the corridor, and the smell was foul," added Targon, pinching his nose.

"Hmm," said Varl. "I wonder if Doc or Chip would know what pressurized chemicals are in the canisters."

"Why don't we go and ask them?" suggested Matt. "We promised Snake we'd only be thirty minutes and we've already been forty."

"Okay, but recharge your computer while we're gone," said Varl. "We'll need to pull up the next set of game instructions tonight. I found this adapter among Chip's computer parts. It should fit your laptop."

Targon pulled himself off the mattress and stood up. He stretched his arms above his head. "How many hours before bed? I'm always confused when there's no natural light."

Matt looked at his digital watch. "It's only 4 p.m. Plenty of time to find information about the Vorgs *and* sort out our next plan of attack."

"Let's get to work. We've got plenty to do," said Varl. He smiled to himself as he followed the boys out of his room. It was great to have them back. Already his adrenaline was pumping. Matt and Targon made him feel young and alive . . . and needed.

* * * * *

Matt watched from the doorway as Angel chatted excitedly to the group gathered in the kitchen. He had never seen her look happier. Her red curls bounced with the movement of her head as she recounted her dramatic escape. Two large dimples enhanced her wide smile. She pushed up the sleeves of her lacy blouse and leaned on the table, rolling her bright green eyes and exaggerating her movements when she got to the scary part of her ordeal. Fly couldn't seem to take his eyes off his sister.

When she was done, there was silence in the room. Matt looked at Bee, Chip, Doc, Snake and Fly. Not one of them moved. It was as if they couldn't quite comprehend how the three of them could have stolen an airbug and lived to tell the tale.

"Did you tell them the part about the canisters?" asked Targon.

"Only briefly," said Angel.

"I think you all ought to hear more about this," said Varl in a serious tone. "From what the boys have told me, it seems we may have found the Vorgs' weakness."

Chip sat up in his chair. "How so?"

"It seems that the Vorgs were blinded—at least temporarily—by whatever was in those canisters."

"I'm guessing they're Govan fire extinguishers," said Matt.

Doc nodded and cleared his throat. "The canisters contain Capriclan. This is a combination of two chemicals, easily made in any laboratory, which will douse a fire within seconds. The purple mist given off by the pressurized release from the canister is not harmful to human lungs or eyes."

"Is it possible that the Vorgs' eyes are so different from ours that Capriclan could blind them but not hurt us?" asked Chip.

"The Vorgs' strength, lethal venom, and ability to regenerate body parts suggests that they are genetically very different from lizards indigenous to *this* planet," said Doc. He adjusted his glasses on the bridge of his nose. "Once we have Xandix III working, I should be able to do more research and provide better answers."

Varl patted Doc on the back. "I think Chip and I had better get back to work. It's imperative that we get the Xandix network up and running as soon as possible."

"I'll say," agreed Matt. "While you two are working on that, I'll check out my computer program, okay?"

Chip was already on his way out of the room. Varl nodded in agreement and took two steps after him. He hesitated at the door and turned to face Doc. "Could *you* make Capriclan, Doc?"

Doc smiled. "With the right equipment and adequate supplies of Capric 76 and Lanqua K . . . sure."

Matt picked up some uncertainty in Doc's tone. He sighed. "There's a 'but' coming, isn't there?"

Varl smiled at Matt. "*But*, Doc, you're about to tell us that neither chemical is easy to get, and you don't have a laboratory here in the caves."

Doc removed his glasses, folded them carefully and

placed them inside his jacket pocket. He pursed his lips. "You understand the situation perfectly," he replied, frowning. "Without access to a state-of-the-art lab, like the one in Bay City University, it would be virtually impossible."

Varl rubbed his chin. "Write a list of everything you would need and where we might find it, will you?"

Doc nodded. "Willingly—but I don't think it will do much good. I'll be surprised if you can find half the things."

Varl didn't reply. He just grinned and rushed after Chip.

"Don't be so sure," Matt said to Doc. "You'd be surprised what Varl can come up with."

Chapter 13

Jesper's hissed a well-known Vorg tune as he flew the airbug toward Bay City University Technology Complex. His spirits had been lifted by the information he had just learned from Urg. Things were beginning to connect.

He set the airbug down in a field behind the university. The tall bushes at the edge of the field would help camouflage the vehicle at ground level. The bug would be easier to spot from the air, but there was nothing he could do about that. He hoped that its dark green color would blend in with the lushness of the grass and bushes.

Jesper set off toward the back entrance of the Technology Complex and glanced back several times just to be sure that the airbug wasn't obvious to passersby. Until he could prove his theory about the fate of the missing airbug, he needed to keep his investigation a secret. He felt a rush of excitement. Gubala would soon realize his mistake and have to take back his rebuke. Jesper grinned happily. He would be respected by Gubala for his ingenuity, receive a promotion for his work, and Harless and Yorak would look like idiots.

Jesper looked up at the abandoned Technology Complex. The hexagonal blue glass windows glinted in the sun invitingly, but there was an eerie stillness as he approached the steps to the lower level. Jesper heaved open the door, careful not to cut himself on the smashed panes of glass. He wondered why his Vorg colleagues, who had been sent to destroy the computer systems, had broken everything else as well. "Wanton vandalism," he muttered. "No need for such deliberate destruction."

In every classroom and laboratory he passed, equipment had been destroyed, chairs and tables turned over, and computer software thrown across the floor.

Jesper needed information about Gova. What better place to get it than from the Govans' own data bases? He knew exactly what he was looking for, but was unsure where to find it. He entered one of the labs. This seemed as good a place to start as any. One or two computer monitors remained intact, but the cables had been ripped out and all of the computers smashed. He realized instantly that none of them would work.

"Such stupidity," he growled. "A wealth of information at our fingertips about this entire empire, and we destroyed it all."

Jesper made his way back into the corridor and into the laboratory next door. Not a single piece of equipment had been spared destruction. He snarled his disgust. At the back of the room, shelves of software had been tipped over. Thousands of files lay strewn across the floor. He crawled on his knees reading the labels. There were files of information on everything from Govan genetics to biological experiments performed at the university over the last three decades. "I need geography or physical features of the land," he muttered.

He looked around at the glass containers and bottles broken on the benches. These were the science labs. He was in the wrong classroom. There had to be other rooms in the complex where students learned topography and geology.

Jesper climbed the stairs to the second level. The narrow steps were not designed for feet his size. He lost his footing several times before reaching the top. A large sign, *Geography Department,* greeted him. Jesper smiled. Now perhaps he would find what he needed.

In the geography lab, the benches were smooth and empty of equipment. Racks of charts had been pulled over by his comrades. Jesper picked a chart from the pile and spread it across the lab bench. It showed land contours to the north of Bay City. It was not what he wanted. He needed maps of the terrain near the coast.

He allowed the roll to spring closed and opened another. By the time he reached the tenth chart, he was agitated. Surely there were topographical maps of the coast.

Jesper's heart raced as he caught a glimpse of blue on the edge of the next roll. Quickly he spread out the chart. "Bay City Nature Preserve," he laughed. "Exactly what I want. Now I'm getting somewhere."

Jesper studied the detailed computer drawing. The cliffs to the south were sheer and the rock type was perfect for caves, but none were shown on the map. He clenched the paper in his claws and growled. His gut told him that he was on the right track even though the maps said otherwise. Thermal imaging equipment would solve the mystery once and for all. It was stored in the shed on The Factory roof. How would he get it and leave no record of it being checked out?

"Urg will help me without question," he muttered.

He thought briefly about calling him, but it was too risky. Since his run-in with Harless and Yorak, it was likely that his calls were being monitored. The ambitious self-seekers were out to secure his downfall and would do anything to get rid of him permanently. He had to be patient. He would pay Urg a visit at dusk and see if he could borrow the thermal imaging equipment without signing for it. If everything went according to plan, he would have it back in the shed before dawn and no one would be any the wiser.

* * * * *

Varl put the last of the tiny computer components back into the box. He sat back with satisfaction. They were done. He and Chip had labored solidly for several hours on the Xandix III system, and now they were ready to put their work to the test.

Chip wiped the sweat off his forehead with a handkerchief. "It seems hot in here."

"Nerves," replied Varl. "I'm as anxious as you. Let's see if our efforts have paid off."

Chip shoved his handkerchief back in his pocket and touched a small button on the top of the Xandix III cube. A green light on the top flashed twice. The gentle hum that followed was a welcome sound. Varl slapped Chip on the back. "Success!" he shouted. "I knew that two good brains could have this system working again in no time."

"Not so fast," said Chip. "Just because Xandix III boots up doesn't mean the system will work."

"Well, what are you waiting for?" asked Varl. "Put on the helmet, key in the password, access the files, and let's see whether or not the network is still intact."

"You seem more excited than I am to get this running," Chip marveled.

Varl smiled. The Xandix computer system might play a vital part in winning Matt's computer game. They had to get it working and find out all they could about the Vorgs. "I love a scientific challenge," he said as a cover for his eagerness.

Chip pulled the helmet over his head and sat on a stool in front of the monitor. Instantly a menu appeared on the large screen. Chip made selections and scrolled through files without a word. Varl watched in awe. The elimination of a keyboard and a microphone added a new dimension to computing. A computer with the ability to read thoughts and act instantly did away with so much of the frustration associated with accessing and downloading information. A red star flashed in the left corner of the sky-blue screen.

"Entering the network now," announced Chip. "If we've been successful, and if our trimods and optics have not been discovered by the Vorgs, we should have a visual anywhere in Bay City within a few seconds."

Varl bit his lip. He could hardly contain his excitement. He'd seen firsthand the technology of an advanced computer system. He could learn so much from these people that he could take back and use in Zaul.

"Success!" said Chip, unable to hide his relief. "Xandix shows that all trimods are functioning."

"There's a trimod in each room of every building linked to the network, correct?" said Varl.

Chip nodded. "A hundred optics in the walls transmit images and sounds to the trimod in that room, and the trimod then sends its information through the network. Here we go. Let's try trimod HD 1. That's the main lobby of the Health Department."

"Impressive."

"I'll bring up the trimods in the Bay City government offices and the university."

Varl watched in awe as Chip switched from trimod to trimod all over the city. The pictures were clear. Chip showed how he could use the optics to provide a complete view of every room. Vorgs were in many of the buildings, and their conversations were clearly audible through the enormous speakers underneath the screen.

"This is incredible!" said Varl.

"Now we're viewing the university," announced Chip.

"This is the Sports Complex. I'm switching to trimod SC 2. We'll scan the optics. This is optic 12 and now optic 13 . . ."

"There are two Vorgs in the entrance," Varl muttered as Chip changed the camera angle yet again. "This is great being able to watch their activities. What a system!"

Chip continued flicking from trimod to trimod. "This is the Technology Complex. Optics 14, 15 and 16—there's a Vorg in this room too. Now the Math Studies Department . . .."

"Go back," shouted Varl. "Go back to the Technology Complex. I think you were on trimod TC 10, optic 16."

"What did you see?" asked Chip.

"Find it, quickly," snapped Varl. "There, hold it there! The Vorg in the picture—I recognize him. I can't believe I'm saying that, but there's no doubt about it. That Vorg is the Commander of The Factory. His distinctive purple cloak is permanently fixed in my memory . . . I'm sure it's him."

"What's his name?"

"I seem to remember he called himself Jesper of the Mount. Why do you suppose he's looking at charts in the university's Technology Complex?"

Chip shrugged. "Let's see if we can get a closer look at the chart. I'll change to optic 19 and focus on the map."

Varl froze. He looked at Chip, whose face had

turned white. "It's a coastal map of this area, isn't it?"

Chip nodded.

"Why do you suppose he'd be interested in the topography of the coast?" asked Varl.

Chip yanked off the helmet and pushed back the stool. His face looked gaunt and drained. He gulped. "Only one reason I can think of. The Vorgs must have somehow tracked the airbug here, and they're confused by its disappearance into the cliff."

"I thought there wasn't a tracking system on non-military bugs," said Varl.

"There isn't—but it is the only explanation I can think of."

"Any Vorg standing on the cliffs would have seen the airbug approaching the coast and reported it," Varl deduced.

"Quite probable. I'd better let the others know. If Jesper of the Mount has an ounce of intelligence, it won't be long before he figures out that the Resistance has made its base in the old cliff lookout."

"Then our days here will be numbered," muttered Varl.

* * * * *

Targon sat close to Matt on the mattress. He was beginning to recognize certain words that appeared on the computer screen. "That says '*Menu*'," he announced proudly.

Matt smiled. "You're doing great. You'll soon be reading everything."

"We've found out about the Resistance and about how to attack the Vorgs. What's the next step?" asked Targon.

"Now we need to find out about the Keeper," Matt replied. He scrolled down the menu until he reached number 9, '*The Keeper,*' and pointed to it on the screen.

"Thanks," said Targon. "It's a word I won't forget." He shuddered, remembering his past encounters with the Keeper in the first two levels of Matt's game. "What or who do you think the Keeper will be this time?"

Matt shrugged. "Your guess is as good as mine, but I like the idea that the Keeper has to be activated and not destroyed in this level."

"That doesn't mean that it will be any easier to *find* the Keeper," said Targon.

"Agreed. But it's a neat twist to the game, don't you think? Here goes," said Matt, locking the cursor on number 9 and pressing '*Enter*'. "Let's see if we can work out the rhyme."

Targon gazed in awe at the brilliant picture of a night sky that appeared on the screen. "That's so beautiful," he said with a deep sigh. Millions of stars twinkled on a black background. The accompanying tinkling music was peaceful.

"Here's the rhyme," said Matt. "Do you want to try and read it?"

Targon shook his head. "Don't think I'm quite ready

for that. If you point to the words, I'll follow along."

"Better still, I'll click on *'Audio'* and the rhyme will be read to us."

A high-pitched feminine voice sang the words.

> To find the Keeper look to space
> Beyond this galaxy is the Vorgan race
> Space travel is not your game
> Old technology will find its fame
> Be precise with date and time
> Prevent a continued Vorgan line
> Sad it seems, but you must not fail
> Activate the Keeper to prevail.

Matt stared at the words on the screen. He said nothing.

"Sorry, I don't have any bright ideas this time," said Targon. "It's pretty creepy, though."

"Well, we know the Vorgs are from another planet, so the first two lines are clear. We're not going to be traveling into space, that's also clear."

"It's telling us to use *old* technology," said Targon. "Varl would find that amusing. What's old to us is modern to you. A spacecraft, perhaps?"

Matt shook his head. "The rhyme wouldn't say to be precise with date and time if it's something we can't control, and if we're not traveling ourselves, it's unlikely to be a spacecraft."

"Then what?" asked Targon. "It sounds as though

this old technology *is* the Keeper. Do you think it's some kind of missile we have to activate and send to destroy the planet Vorgus?"

Matt's face brightened. He jumped off the mattress excitedly. "Great going, Targon! I'll bet you anything it's the EDS Program!" he shouted.

"It's what?" asked Targon. He felt totally lost by Matt's latest conclusion.

"I bet the riddle is referring to the Earth Defense System!"

"What's that?" Targon asked again.

"I'll explain later," said Matt, dragging him through the door. "Right now, we need to find Varl. He'll know whether or not EDS is still up there. It's been five hundred years since the system was developed, but I'll bet you anything it's still in orbit!"

Matt raced down the tunnel toward the computer room. Targon ran after him, barely able to keep up. They turned the corner and ran smack into Varl and Chip.

"Whoa! You'll knock over an old man going at that speed!" exclaimed Varl. "What's the rush, boys?" He chuckled as he rubbed his forehead.

"EDS!" gasped Matt.

"ED what?" asked Varl

"EDS technology. You know—it was being developed in 2009—the Earth Defense System. You haven't heard of it?"

"Yes, I know a little about it," replied Varl. "It was the first *global* defense system. Several nations worked together to develop a method of protecting the Earth from an asteroid collision."

Matt was bent over at the waist, gasping for air.

Targon decided to continue while Matt regained his breath.   He knew that he had to be careful how he discussed the latest *Keeper of the Kingdom* riddle in front of Chip and the others. They knew nothing of Matt's computer game, and it would be better if it stayed that way. "We can *activate* EDS, if it is still in orbit," he said, hoping that Varl would understand his choice of words and realize that he was referring to the riddle.

Varl smiled as if he had grasped the meaning. He put his arm around Targon's shoulders. "I can see that Matt has been doing some research on his computer." He winked.   "EDS might be very useful to prevent more Vorgs from settling here."

Matt stood up and breathed in deeply. "That was my thought exactly."

"Is it . . .is it really likely that more Vorgs will come?" Targon stammered.

"Very," Chip replied, sporting a grim expression. "It's my guess that the several hundred Vorgs here at the moment are just the scouting group for millions of others that will follow. I suspect that spacecraft will begin landing daily once the Vorgs think they have complete control." He sighed.

"UFOs," mumbled Targon. "That's what Matt and I saw in the cornfield. I'll bet anything it was a Vorg spacecraft."

"Later today we'll investigate the possibility of using the old EDS technology to prevent more Vorgs from arriving," Varl concluded.

"Later today? Why not now?" asked Matt.

"Because something more pressing has occurred," said Chip. "Let's keep going. We must get the others together immediately."

"What's happened that's so urgent?" asked Targon, treading on Chip's heels.

"We got the Xandix III working," replied Varl.

"Well, that's good, isn't it?" said Targon, trying to talk as they kept up a brisk pace. "Now we can spy on the Vorgs."

"Exactly," said Varl. "That's what we did—and we didn't like what we saw."

Chapter 14

"So that's the situation," said Chip firmly. "We've been honest with you all. It's grim. Our cliff homes could be attacked by Vorgs at any time."

The B family dining room was crowded but silent. Matt looked around at the group gathered around the table. Doc, Chip and Varl bore serious expressions. Bee hurried in and out of the kitchen providing evening drinks and snacks as if the gathering were for a festive occasion. Spider kept looking at Varl's new pants and shirt, admiring her work, obviously not very concerned with the news.

Angel sat on a bench in the corner, her face giving nothing away about her feelings. Fly's arm was draped loosely over her shoulder in a protective manner. Snake stood next to Targon, broadly grinning as if he couldn't wait for the excitement that was about to begin.

"Preparations to combat the Vorgs must be intensified. We must work around the clock," added Doc in a tone befitting a general about to lead a military campaign.

Varl sat down at the end of the table and cleared his throat. "We will begin preparation later tonight under the cover of darkness. I hope you will all do your jobs with the utmost seriousness. Beating the Vorgs requires a combined effort. Once we are prepared, we will have to join forces with the other families in the cliff homes. Nine of us against four or five hundred Vorgs is obviously ridiculous."

"Thank goodness you said that," said Bee, wiping her face with her apron. "I was beginning to think you were all mad." She stood still for the first time since the beginning of the meeting and focused on what Varl was saying.

"What have you got planned?" asked Matt, eager to discover how Varl was proposing to play out the clues from the rhymes in the computer game.

Varl cleared his throat. "The first priority is to attack the Vorgs at their Achilles' heel—their weakness. Doc has briefly researched Vorg genetics and has discovered that Capriclan blinds Vorg eyes, often causing permanent damage. It is the perfect weapon."

Matt smiled. Targon had done well with his observations.

Doc adjusted his glasses. "I will lead the first phase of our plan. Matt, Snake, Angel and Fly will gather enough chemicals and equipment for me to make large quantities of Capriclan. This will be a dangerous task. If anyone doesn't wish to take part, I will understand."

Angel and Fly looked at each other briefly. They answered in unison, "We're with you, Doc."

Snake nodded his head in agreement. "Fine by me."

Chip rubbed his balding head briskly. "As you know, the Xandix III is now working again."

Everyone applauded and cheered.

Chip laughed and bowed several times. He composed himself and continued. "While the ingredients for making Capriclan are being gathered, Varl has research to do, and Targon, Bee and Spider will take turns observing the Vorgs around the clock. We need to know anything and everything about these creatures, their habits and their weaknesses. When it comes time to use Capriclan, we want to be able to use it effectively."

Matt watched Targon's face brighten. Targon was so observant, it was the perfect job for him.

"Once the Capriclan has been made and research done, we'll move on to Phase II of our plan," said Varl. "The second phase will be difficult. Matt and Snake, I hope you're with me on this. We are going to do what we can to activate the old Earth Defense System and prevent more Vorgs from arriving. "Angel and Targon will be needed as emergency rescue with the airbug. Doc and Chip could pilot the bug, but in my opinion they will be needed here to coordinate. This will be a dangerous mission." Varl looked around at Matt. "Everyone game?"

Matt was delighted. "I wouldn't miss it for anything," he responded, thankful that Varl realized the importance of what he had told him about EDS less than an hour earlier.

"Okay, mate. Sounds good," said Snake, rubbing his hands together.

Angel tossed back her hair and laughed. "Back in the cockpit? Sure. I'll be a professional pilot in no time. You can count on me as backup and Targon will be my navigator."

Targon pursed his lips together and shrugged his shoulders. "I've done it once; I can do it again."

Matt went over the words of the rhyme in his mind. The Earth Defense System *had* to exist. He couldn't think of any other old technology capable of destroying incoming spacecraft. *Please may it not have turned into a piece of space junk,* he prayed.

"Any questions?" asked Varl.

No one spoke. Several shook their heads.

Varl smiled. "Good. Let's get to it. Good luck everyone."

"One more thing," said Chip. "Be careful. Take no chances. The Vorgs are highly dangerous. This is no game."

Matt shot a glance at Targon, who grinned back at him. *If only they knew.*

As the room emptied, Varl beckoned to Matt and Snake. He unrolled a map and laid it on the table.

Snake immediately placed his grubby forefinger in the center of the chart. "That's the spaceport."

"Correct," said Varl. "The spaceport is on this side of Bay City, but inland. That's where we're heading."

"I can lead you down the sewers 'alfway. But then we'll 'ave to be above ground and out in the open."

"I thought we'd be vulnerable for a good part of the journey," said Varl. "I'm glad you were able to clarify that point, Snake, before I put together a plan of action."

"Angel said that airbugs are not allowed near the

spaceport, except for those bringing in workers. Only incoming and outgoing spacecraft can land, which means that we won't have to worry about being seen from the air when we leave the sewers," said Matt.

"Good. That's helpful information," said Varl.

"What are we doin' when we get to the spaceport?"

Varl pointed toward the computer room. "I've got research to do using the Xandix III before I can tell you that. EDS was an advanced laser defense system. I'm guessing that we'll be able to tap into the computer system at the spaceport and turn those lasers on incoming Vorg spacecraft."

Snake looked horrified. "But the spaceport is swarmin' with Vorgs!"

"Indeed. There's no question we could be caught. The Vorgs need the massive computer systems in spaceport control to bring in their craft. I'm banking on that fact. Every other computer in the Bay City area has been smashed." Varl turned to look at Matt. "What are your thoughts, Matt, my boy?"

"It's not going to be easy," Matt muttered. "Not only have we got to distract the Vorgs, but we've got to have enough time to play with an unknown computer system and set definite coordinates for the missiles."

Varl nodded. "I'm counting on Doc making some Capriclan canisters for us to take for defense against the Vorgs. Chip knows the spaceport computers well. He worked in the control room before the Vorgs arrived. He'll help me understand the computer system before we set off."

"Okay," said Matt. "I guess we'd better go and help with the search for Capriclan chemicals. We'll see you later."

"You'll be going to the university laboratories. Be careful, Matt. You too, Snake."

As Snake left the room, Matt turned back to Varl and whispered, "Isn't everyone forgetting one thing?"

"What's that, Matt, my boy?"

"We've got to get rid of the Vorgs that are already here, not just prevent more from coming. Capriclan will only blind them."

"And you're right," agreed Varl. "I hadn't overlooked that fact. Capriclan may not be the perfect weapon, but it's all we have right now. Let's not panic the others. I'll talk to Chip and Doc about a backup plan."

Matt bit his bottom lip. "And just when I thought this was all beginning to come together."

* * * * *

Jesper of the Mount hated airbugs. Like everything else humans had designed, they were too small for Vorgs. He squeezed into the cockpit alongside Urg and took the controls.

"I appreciate your help in getting a thermal imager," he said as they lifted off from the roof of The Factory. "When this is all over, and the Great Leader recognizes his mistake in demoting me, I'll make sure you also receive a promotion."

Urg hissed. "Anything to repay those humans for what they did to Renx. He's a good Vorg. He never hurt humans unnecessarily. Treated them with as much respect and kindness as his job would allow. Look what they did to him in return. He'll never see again."

"Humans are like Vorgs. They are only looking for a way to survive. You can't blame them for that. Has Harless removed the canisters from the walls of The Factory?" asked Jesper.

Urg snarled, revealing his upper teeth. "He's a stupid one. No. The canisters remain on the walls. I personally suggested they were a hazard."

"What did he say?"

"He told me not to worry, and that humans won't try the same thing twice."

Jesper laughed. "His stupidity will be his end."

Urg snarled again. "Harless claims that humans are better supervised now than they were when you were in command of The Factory, and that another escape won't happen."

"It would take just one brave human to grab a canister and blind another Vorg. I am sure that Harless knows that, but has chosen to leave the canisters on the walls to remind everyone of my incompetence," said Jesper.

"Will you recommend to Gubala that the canisters be removed?"

"What, and save Harless' neck? Not on your life! I

hope *more* humans escape. I'll be first in line to gloat when he's demoted, and I get my old job back."

"You haven't told me where we are going," said Urg.

"The coast. I have a hunch. If I'm right, the thermal imager will prove my theory."

"Since the imager detects body warmth, even in the dark, I'd say you'll be looking for humans on the cliffs," guessed Urg.

"Not *on* the cliffs, *in* the cliffs."

"What?"

"The imager is so powerful, it can detect the heat of a human up to one hundred feet deep in the rock."

Urg's yellow eyes seemed to cross. "Are you suggesting there might be caves, inhabited by humans, in Bay City Nature Preserve?"

Jesper hissed. "There are none shown on the topographical maps of the area, but I'll bet my life on it. We're nearly there. Turn on the imager. I'll pass over the cliffs and hover close to the rock face."

"*Over* the cliffs?" growled Urg.

Jesper ignored his comment. He knew that Urg hated heights, but he needed his help. "Let me know what you see. Here we go." He steered the bug over the cliff and down to the crashing shore. His stomach tightened. The cliffs were also his least favorite place in Bay City, and yet here he was for the second time in two days. He hovered low at first, almost touching the waves.

Urg scanned the machine slowly across the rock through the open side of the airbug. The imager shook in his arms. "Nothing detected at this level. Climb fifty feet."

Jesper opened the vertical thrusters, and they rose up the cliff face. "How about here?"

"Possible. Slight readings. Try a little higher."

Jesper steered midway up the cliff. He paused and waited. His heart raced. "Anything?"

Urg grunted. "Definite hot spots. Seems to be one large area and other little ones. That's strange . . ."

"What? Tell me!" hissed Jesper.

"The large area has just broken up into smaller ones. They seem to be moving in every direction."

"Those are humans," said Jesper with satisfaction. "I knew it. Save the results—we'll print them out later. I've got one more thing to do before I can prove to Gubala where the Resistance is hiding."

Chapter 15

M att followed Snake through the sewers, calf-deep in water. They had all rolled up their pants above the knees and taken off their shoes. He caught his breath as he slipped on the bottom of the huge drain. Snake carried the only flashlight and the near-darkness made their journey more difficult. Matt marveled at the speed with which his new friend navigated his way around the stinking tunnels.

Angel complained constantly, but in a humorous tone. "Who's not washed this morning?" she said for the second time.

"Your first joke, 'Caught any skunks lately?' was better," retorted Fly.

"Sorry if my jokes are bad," she snapped. "I'm just trying to pass the time in this awful stench."

"You'll get used to it," shouted Snake from the front.

Angel groaned. "I've been walking in this for at least thirty minutes, and I haven't got used to it yet. Don't know how you can spend so much time down here."

"I'm good at navigating in the dark, just like you seem to be good at piloting airbugs," replied Snake. "People enjoy what they're good at."

Don't know how anyone can enjoy this, thought Matt. He knew that Angel's complaining was not just about the smell of the sewers. Before they had set out, Chip had given each of them a haircut to blend in with the desensitized humans on the streets of Bay City—all except for Fly, whose head was already shaved. There was little Chip could do to change the teenager's appearance. Matt hated the chili-bowl haircut he now sported, but it was necessary. For Angel to give up her lovely locks of ginger hair must have been hard, but she agreed without argument to have it cut. Matt had watched her bravely stifle the tears when she saw her curls lying on the kitchen floor.

Spider had dug into her box of fabric scraps and cut-up old clothes. In a couple of hours she had thrown together drab outfits for each of them, similar to the one that Varl had taken from the old man in Bay City. At least they were comfortable, even if the style was plain.

Matt struggled to keep his bag out of the water. Fly carried a second bag. The chemicals they needed to collect from the university would be in a powder form and would have to be kept completely dry. Even though the bags were made of a thick plastic, he worried about getting water inside through the open top. He worried even more about the journey back, when the bag would be full of chemicals.

"We're going up," announced Snake, his feet already on the first rungs of a ladder. "Take it easy. It's a long climb, and the bars are slippery."

Matt clutched the handles of the bag tightly. It wasn't easy to hold onto both the ladder and the bag.

It was a cloudless night. The moon was no longer full, but it shed enough light from the grid above to illuminate the top of the ladder. Matt was pleased to smell fresh air. Snake heaved open the grid, clambered out and helped him onto the street.

"Run for that building," he whispered, pointing to a tall glass tower about fifty yards away.

Matt did as instructed. He crouched in the entrance, waiting for the others, and searched for any sign of Vorgs. It had been wise to plan this raid at night. Vorgs liked their sleep as much as humans. To get to the Technology Complex at the university they would have to pass through the eastern edge of Bay City. The return journey in daylight would be more hazardous.

Angel joined Matt in the shadows. She crouched low and ran her fingers through her shorn hair.

"It looks great, Angel," Matt whispered. "You notice your green eyes more when your hair is short."

She smiled at him. "Thanks, but you don't have to be nice. I know it looks terrible. We all look terrible."

Matt sighed. He had never been good at giving compliments to girls. He really had meant what he said, but there'd be no convincing her.

Fly ran across the street, closely followed by Snake.

"Okay. We're all 'ere. Follow me, mates," said Snake, barely pausing to take a breath. "Stay in the shadows." He set off at a fast pace, somewhere between a jog and a sprint.

Matt was panting before he had covered half the

distance to the university. He looked around cautiously.
The streets were silent at 4 a.m., but there would be Vorg
patrols to watch for.   Vorgs could materialize without
notice in one of the many chambers erected on the street
corners. He stopped at the corner of Bryant and Main
streets, his eyes unable to avoid staring into the
materialization chamber positioned there.   Matt
shuddered and looked over his shoulder before darting
across the street after Snake and the others. At least
airbug lights could easily be seen at night and there
would be plenty of warning before one set down. His
heart was still pounding when he reached the Technology
Complex doors.

"Thought you were fit," rebuked Angel. "We've been
waiting five minutes."

"That's an exaggeration," snapped Matt.

"Let's go. We've got plenty to do," said Snake,
pulling open the battered door. He gasped as he saw the
shards of glass cluttering the hallway. "Wow! Them
Vorgs really made a mess of the place."

Glass crunched under Matt's feet as he made his
way along the corridor. He felt along the walls in the
dark. Snake had turned off the flashlight in case Vorg
patrols saw the beam through the windows.

"In 'ere," said Snake, turning into the first classroom.
"We'll sit on the floor and wait until dawn."

"The sun will be up in less than an hour," said Matt.
He crawled under one of the lab benches and closed his
eyes.

Time passed slowly. Matt nodded off occasionally but couldn't get comfortable on the cold floor. Slowly, daylight began to filter through the windows. Bird songs announced the arrival of a new day. Matt yawned.

"Okay," said Snake. "Let's do what we gotta do."

"Stay away from the windows," Matt reminded him. He stood up and stretched his arms. "Angel and Fly, you collect the computer components and scrap pieces that Doc wanted. The metal shop is on this floor—rooms 60 to 64. We'll see you back here. Snake, come with me. We've got to find hydrogen peroxide and the chemicals."

"We've got thirty minutes and no more," said Snake.

Matt crept along the corridor to the next lab. His heart sank as he walked in. A mess of chemicals and containers covered the floor. It would be hard to find what they were looking for.

"Capric 76," whispered Snake. He held up a plastic container with traces of a deep blue powder at the bottom.

"Good start," mouthed Matt, "but that's not nearly enough."

A heavy wooden door at the back of the room caught his attention. "Equipment Store, it has to be," he muttered, making his way around the smashed stools strewn across the floor. "Most school biology and chemistry labs back home have them."

The door was already ajar. Matt pushed it open. Many of the items had been swept off the shelves and had spilled when they hit the floor. Matt reached for the containers still on the shelves, moving bottles aside to read all the labels. The acrid smell burned the inside of his nose. He pinched his nostrils and continued.

A large white label with bright red letters, Lanqua K, faced him. The container was almost full of a crimson powder. His heart raced with excitement. Now all he needed was more Capric to go with the small quantity that Snake had found. On the second shelf nearly every container was labeled Capric. His initial excitement turned to despair when he realized that Capric came in many forms. He moved one jar after another. *Capric 23, Capric 29, Capric 44. What is this stuff?*

On the lower shelf, the containers of Capric were half used. Matt was beginning to think they would have to be content with a smaller quantity of Capric, when in the corner of the cupboard his glance fell on a label, Capric 76. He could see through the clear plastic that the container was nearly full. He felt like dancing.

He grabbed the Lanqua K and Capric 76, shut the storeroom door, and walked to the front of the room where Snake was still searching for hydrogen peroxide. "Any luck?" Matt asked, placing the two containers on the lab bench.

Snake shook his head.

"There's none in the storeroom either. Doc said we must have it. Hydrogen peroxide is the active ingredient. Water won't do."

"I think there are other labs," said Snake.

Matt put the containers in the black bag and followed

him into the science lab across the corridor.

"Do you think this stuff will do?" asked Snake, lifting up a huge bottle with clear liquid.

Matt shook his head. "Totally different stuff. I know that from biology. That's formaldehyde. It would be fine if you wanted to preserve frogs for dissection!"

"What's that about dissection?" asked Angel, entering the room.

"We're talking about formaldehyde," said Matt.

"Never mind frogs, let's preserve Vorgs and dissect them," said Fly.

Snake shuddered. "Preservation and dissection's not for me. Don't care what them Vorgs 'ave done."

Matt laughed. "Did you find everything, Angel?"

Angel struggled to lift up her bag. The contents clinked together. "There's more here than what Doc asked for."

Fly laughed. "She cleared the shelves."

"We're ready to head back," said Angel, lowering the bag to the floor.

"We just need hydrogen peroxide," said Matt. "What's that bottle on its side by your foot, Snake?"

Snake picked it off the floor. "Nah. It's more formalde'yde."

"Try over there in the corner. That brown cupboard," said Angel.

The doors were ajar. Snake sorted through the bottles on the shelves. "Bingo! Peroxide—and it's new."

"Is there another one?" asked Matt. "One won't go

far."

Matt searched the floor, picking up overturned items and putting them back on the shelves as he ruled them out. "Check every bottle on the floor," he instructed the others. "Lots of containers rolled under the benches."

Next to him, under a stool, lay a large bottle. Before he could read the label he heard the building's outer doors close, followed by a familiar hissing noise. "Vorgs! Hide!"

Angel ducked down next to him under the bench. She put her hand over her mouth and stared at him with wide eyes. Matt listened intently. He heard the Vorgs' heavy footsteps as they crunched across a floor strewn with glass and debris. He listened to their conversation.

"What's of interest here, sir?"

"The History Department on the second floor."

Angel shook noticeably. The Vorgs passed by the classroom. Matt heard them conversing and laughing in deep guttural tones. He could tell by their slower steps that they were climbing the stairs.

Matt mouthed, "It's okay." He motioned to Angel to stay put and crept out from under the bench. He needed to know what was of value to a Vorg in the History Department. Deep down he already knew the answer, but Varl and Chip would want proof, for sure.

Angel grabbed his shirt and tried to pull him back, but he shoved her hand off and continued. When he reached the door of the lab, he realized that Angel was on his heels. She gave him a defiant smile that said she was not going to be left behind.

Matt nodded reluctantly and led the way into the corridor. He stepped as carefully as he could between the shards of glass and broken chairs. His feet crunched on something he hadn't seen at the base of the stairs. He froze momentarily. *What am I doing? Do I really want to be desensitized? This is madness.*

Matt reached the top step. He crept along the corridor to where the voices became loud, and pressed his back against the wall, staying away from the classroom door. Angel tiptoed alongside.

"Look for anything to do with the history of Bay City Preserve, Urg."

"What time period, Jesper, sir?"

"Not sure. I'm interested in the cliff formations. Archeology . . . history of things found during archeological digs—anything that gives us a clue about caves."

"Here's something. It's a research paper—*Cliff Defense during the 26th Century: The Value of Maintaining the Cliff Caves,* by R. W. Dodd."

"Unbelievable. That's better than I had hoped for—almost too easy."

"Gubala will have to listen to you when he sees this," Urg chuckled. "Yorak of the Vale was told to locate the Resistance. He'll be the next one to suffer the wrath of the Great Leader."

Jesper hissed. "Serves him right, the arrogant Vorg. Since we arrived, he's spent more time catering to

Gubala's every need than doing his job."

"Are we heading straight to the Great Complex?" Urg asked.

Jesper snorted. "Not yet. I want to read this document carefully and present Gubala with facts, not just supposition."

The conversation died. Papers rustled. Matt realized they were about to leave. Panic set in. He had been stupid. Where could he and Angel run without being heard? The doors in this corridor were all closed. They would have to go back down the stairs. He tugged Angel's arm and leaped away from the wall. Angel sprinted after him. He raced down, taking two steps at a time, almost sliding down in his haste.

"Humans!" Urg hollered in his deep voice.

Matt stumbled, tripping over his own feet near the bottom of the stairs. Fly and Snake were already in the corridor. Each held a black bag containing the vital chemicals and components. Snake headed for the main doors, the metal pieces clinking together as he ran. Matt ran down the corridor, and tore through the exit into the daylight. He hesitated outside, waiting for Angel.

The Vorgs were at the top of the stairs, hissing and snarling.

"You go, I'll wait for my sister," said Fly, holding the door open. "The Vorgs' huge feet make them slow on the stairs." He thrust the black bag into Matt's hands.

"Go Fly! Go Matt!" Angel yelled. "I'm coming!"

Fly pushed Matt away from the door. "Get the stuff

back. Go, I tell you! We're all dead without it."

Matt's heart pounded. He looked at Fly's determined face and ran. Angel was only a couple of seconds behind.

As he turned the corner of the building he heard Angel scream. It was a sound of pain—a sound that ripped through his bones and ate at his insides. What had happened? She had been right on his heels.

Without looking back, Matt raced toward the corner of Main and Bryant. He halted next to an empty materialization chamber. The streets were busy. Desensitized humans walked everywhere. He had to compose himself or any Vorgs that materialized would notice him. Matt took a deep breath and strolled like the others with his head high and a dazed look on his face. His heart felt heavy, and tears were ready to burst down his hot cheeks. He fought his emotions. Only the importance of the chemicals he carried kept him going. His eyes focused on the entrance to the sewers in the middle of the street. He was just two minutes from safety. But where was Snake? Without him it would be impossible to find his way back down the labyrinth of tunnels.

Chapter 16

Snake, where are you? Matt stared at the grid in the center of the road as he put one foot in front of the other. He had less than fifty yards to go. *Walk*, he reminded himself. Don't step too quickly. He wanted to turn and check for Vorgs materializing on the street corner behind, but he knew he had to behave like every other desensitized human right up until he lifted that lid and scrambled down the drain.

Four Vorgs suddenly materialized in a chamber on the opposite side of Main Street, and began moving in his direction. Matt eyed them suspiciously. He squeezed between two humans walking in front and maintained the same pace. His heart pounded as the Vorgs grew near. He gently moved the black bag to his other clammy hand, hoping that it would not be as conspicuous. It hadn't taken long for Vorg patrols to be out looking for him. He felt sick as he thought of Angel and Fly on their way to The Factory. That was the fate awaiting him, if he were caught.

He dared to glance briefly across the street, looking for a warning that he had been spotted and would have to run. The Vorgs chatted and joked in a relaxed manner, passing by without incident. They did not seem to be searching for renegade humans. Matt slowed his pace, confused, half-expecting them to come up suddenly behind him. Why were the streets not swarming with Vorgs by now? Hadn't the alarm been sounded that renegades were loose on the streets?

Matt drew close to the sewer entrance. He looked at the metal cover in the road. His eyes glazed. It was less than ten feet from where he stood, yet he couldn't bring himself to run. It was as if the events that had happened in the university had drained his resolve. Thanks to Angel, he had escaped The Factory and found Varl. In return he had abandoned her. His ears hummed, and his head spun. Guilt weighed heavily on his mind.

A woman brushed past him. Matt was quickly brought back to the present. What good would he be to Angel if he allowed himself to be caught? If he managed to get the chemicals back to Doc, then maybe they had a chance of rescuing her. He swallowed hard. *Get a grip, Matt. It's now or never.*

After a brief glance in every direction, Matt sprinted into the street. He placed the bag on the road, and heaved the cover off with both hands. Quickly, he found his footing and slipped inside. It was a struggle to lift the grid back over the opening while holding the bag. Panting, Matt gripped the bag and the ladder with his left hand, and began his descent.

At the bottom, in the dark, he felt safe. His heart slowed. Vorgs would have trouble squeezing through the sewer opening and wouldn't be able to climb down the narrow ladders with their enormous feet. He stood in the filthy water, still wearing his shoes, clutching the precious bag to his chest. Dare he attempt the journey back on his own?

A hand gripped his shoulder. Matt lurched forward in the water, almost dropping the bag. He struggled to regain his balance on the slippery bottom.

"Matt . . . Matt . . . it's me, mate."

Matt felt such relief to hear Snake's distinctive accent. "Thank goodness," he mumbled back, his heart still racing from the shock. "I thought the Vorgs had found a way into the sewers."

"Not yet. Where are Fly and Angel?"

Matt gulped. "They didn't make it." He could see Snake's gangly shape next to him in the half-light.

"I'm sorry," said Snake. "There ain't nothin' we could 'ave done to 'elp them against them Vorgs. I knew you'd all need me to get you 'ome, so I waited 'ere where it was safe."

"It's okay," said Matt hearing Snake's voice quaver. "You did the right thing. Have you got the other bag?"

"Yeah, but I dropped the flashlight."

Matt sighed. "Oh. So what do we do without light?"

"Not a problem," replied Snake. "I know every turn and entrance in this 'ere drain. It'll just take us longer to get 'ome."

Matt grabbed the back of Snake's shirt with his left hand and held the bag tightly with his right. "Okay. What are we waiting for? Let's get these chemicals to Doc."

Together they waded through the cold water, in

darkness and in silence.

* * * * *

Jesper smiled at his good fortune.   He picked the limp body off the floor. Had the girl with the ginger hair not slipped on the broken glass at the entrance to the Technology Complex, she would have been long gone. Instead, his magnificent tongue had ensnared her. The young man with her had surrendered when he witnessed the effects of his venom. He wondered how he might use his two prisoners to his best advantage. Should he take them to The Factory and parade them in front of Yorak and Harless? Should he take them to see Gubala, the Great Leader?

Urg had the young man by the arm. "What do we do with them?" he asked, as if he had read Jesper's thoughts. "Will you take them to The Factory?"

Jesper smiled, allowing the young man to see his pointed front teeth. "First, we get them upstairs. I wish to interrogate them. If we take them straight to The Factory, Harless will desensitize them without a thought. Right now they are more use to me in an alert mental state."

Urg nodded and pulled the young man with the strange hairstyle up the stairs.

Jesper followed, carrying the girl. He looked down at her peaceful face. Urg had described her as a hothead. He wondered what she would be like when the effects of his venom wore off. Uncooperative, he didn't doubt. "In here," he directed. "We'll put them in the storeroom at the back."

Urg opened one of the upper-level classroom doors and wound his way around the smashed furniture. He shoved the young man inside.

Jesper laid the girl gently on the floor. As he stood upright, he looked into the boy's desperate eyes and felt overwhelming pity. His deep brown eyes carried the same look that had been in the yellow eyes of Jesper's own son when he'd left Vorgus—a look that haunted him every day he was away. Eyes told so much. These were eyes begging to know if everything would be okay. Jesper shook his head and abruptly closed the storeroom door. Perhaps Harless was right—he was too soft these days.

He paced outside the storeroom. Vorgs had to survive the destruction of their planet. That was the only reason he was here. The stronger species always survived at the weaker one's expense. Vorgs *had to* dominate. He would do what he had to do to keep save his family from elimination. Humans were the enemy, and time was running out for his own species.

* * * * *

Matt handed Varl his smelly wet clothes and wrapped an enormous towel tightly around his body. He sat down in front of the open oven, shaking with the cold.

Bee gave him a steaming cup of herbal tea. "Drink this and you'll feel a lot better."

Her soothing voice had intended to help, but Matt could not shake off the guilt that he felt for returning without Angel and Fly. He muttered Fly's words: *"Get the stuff back. Go, I tell you! We're all dead without it."*

"What did you say, my boy?" asked Varl. He sat down next to Matt on the bench, and warmed his hands in front of the oven.

"That's the last thing Fly said. He pushed me away from the entrance and told me to get the chemicals back to Doc."

"No one's blaming you for what happened," Bee reassured him. "You did what you could under the circumstances. I'll be back shortly. I'm going to check on Snake. There's plenty more tea if you want it."

"Thanks," said Matt. He enjoyed being mothered for a change.

Varl nodded in agreement. "She's right. Angel and Fly knew the danger when they went on the mission. Fly is Angel's brother. It is natural that he would stay to protect her."

Matt hung his head. "*I* should have stayed, too. Perhaps three or four of us could have overpowered two Vorgs."

Varl patted Matt's knee. "Don't beat yourself up any more. There's nothing you could have done. You know a Vorg's venom can be lethal. If you had stayed to help you would have all been captured. Fly was right. Getting the chemicals back to Doc was imperative." He lowered his voice to a whisper. "Besides, have you forgotten why we are here? If we win your *Keeper of the Kingdom* game, we stand a chance to save everyone. You are just playing out the scenario, so let's get to it and win!"

Matt perked up at the mention of his game. Varl was right, as usual. If they could work out the rhymes, and see the scenario through to a successful end, he would save them all from the Vorgs.

"What did you find out from the Xandix III?" asked Matt.

Varl smiled. "EDS, created and put into orbit in 2009, is now a piece of space junk. Most of the original system was dismantled in the late 2100s because new technology had surpassed its capabilities. What's left floating around in orbit is absolutely useless."

Matt's heart sank. He stared at Varl. "So why the happy face?"

"Because the Earth Defense System was updated several times over the last five hundred years. The original system was replaced by Beta EDS, Gamma, Delta and the latest model—built only thirty years ago—Epsilon EDS."

Matt placed his empty cup on the floor by his feet. He felt revitalized by this news. "Does it still work?" he asked eagerly.

"I believe so. Of course, thirty years is *still* a long time ago. According to Xandix III, Epsilon uses powerful space-based lasers that are extremely accurate. There is no record of EDS Epsilon being removed from the defense system, so we can only assume it is still functional."

"Zang it! That's great news. But we've still got major problems. Never mind getting close enough to the computers, or figuring out how to activate Epsilon, how do we find out the coordinates and times of incoming Vorg spacecraft?"

"That does seem to be the most difficult challenge," Varl agreed. "All we can do is prepare for the mission and hope that the others pick up information from their observations of the Vorgs."

Doc entered the kitchen and helped himself to some herbal tea from the large pot on the stove. He ambled over to the central table and sat down on one of the stools. "I'm sorry to hear about Angel and Fly, but you did well to bring back what you did."

"Is it enough?" asked Matt.

Doc pushed out his lips and nodded his head. "Just about. We're a little short on the hydrogen peroxide, but we can make do. Especially since we're using it in tiny gas bombs. The small amount we have of each substance will go much further."

"Gas bombs?" Matt questioned.

Doc slurped his tea. "We need a way to disperse the Capriclan. I don't have the equipment to make pressurized canisters like the fire extinguishers, so I've come up with an inventive way to release the chemical."

That sounds fine," said Varl. "It will be easier to

control and may end up being more accurate."

"There's one thing I haven't told anyone yet," said Matt. He bit his lip. "We were seen by the Vorgs at the university because I was attempting to listen in on their conversation."

"Did you learn anything of importance?" asked Varl.

Matt nodded. "You're not going to like it."

"Don't hold us in suspense!" shouted Doc.

"The Vorgs know about the cliff homes. They found a report on cliff defense in the History Department, which mentioned the homes directly."

Varl groaned. "Chip and I guessed that Jesper of the Mount would continue with his research until he found us. We'd better issue a warning to everyone."

Doc sat calmly. "We've still got time. It will take them a while to work out how to get to us. The back route into these caves was sealed up long ago, which gives us an advantage."

Varl stood up and patted Matt on the shoulder. "While you recover and Doc works on the Capriclan, I'm going back to the computer room. After I finished the EDS research, Targon took over on the Xandix to watch Vorg movements again. Let's hope that he has more detailed information to give us. I'd rather surprise the Vorgs with an attack than sit here and wait for them to come to us!"

Chapter 17

"Time to interrogate the humans," said Jesper, working himself up to the task with a display of aggression. He stomped his feet loudly, snarled and hissed.

"I've got to go to The Factory," said Urg. "I'm already late for my shift, and Harless will ask questions."

Jesper nodded. "Understood. I'll be fine here. If I decide to leave the youngsters, I'll give them a small dose of venom and paralyze them for a few hours. You *will* keep this quiet for now, won't you?"

Urg growled. "Don't worry. You have my complete loyalty."

Jesper was satisfied with his answer. Urg had already done more than he could have hoped for. "Thanks for your help. I hope that this scheme works out for both of our careers."

Jesper watched Urg leave, then he pumped out his chest, put on a fierce face and hissed loudly as he opened the storeroom door.

The girl had recovered. She sat rigidly next to the young man and stared at Jesper defiantly.

Jesper snarled at them both. The girl didn't flinch. Instead, she spat in his face.

"That's all you're worth, you brute," she sneered.

"Angel, don't antagonize him," whispered Fly. He grabbed her hand.

Jesper was taken aback by her bravado. So her name was Angel. Urg was right—she was a real hothead, but he couldn't help but admire her courage. This was going to be interesting. He looked into her eyes. The hatred he saw pierced through him. *You're getting soft*, he thought. *Ignore it.*

"What were you doing here in the Technology Complex?" Jesper hissed.

"What are *you* doing here?" Angel retorted. "We have every right to be here. You don't. This is *our* home, not yours!" She spat at Jesper a second time.

The boy yanked on her arm. "Don't Angel, please." Angel turned to look at the young man. She pulled her arm away. "What's the difference, Fly? We're dead meat anyway. These creatures have no compassion or consideration for other life-forms. What's this ugly object going to do to me now that he won't do to me later? I might as well tell him what I think while I've got the brains to do it. He's destroyed our home, and taken away our parents, and most of our friends and relatives. What more can he take away?" She turned back to look at Jesper. "You murderer!" she screamed.

Jesper stared at her. Her words cut through him. He looked into the green eyes that glared at him. He had never seen such hatred. What had he become? What was he doing to other thinking, feeling creatures in order to save his own kind?

Jesper staggered backward. The girl had called him a murderer. She considered he had no emotions. She thought of him as an object.

"You do not understand," he replied, choking on every word. "Vorgs are about to die. We are only looking for a way to survive. We are not murderers."

The girl closed her mouth and did not respond with another verbal attack. She seemed stunned by his words. He was showing her another side of Vorgs. Perhaps he could make her see why they were here and that they did have a heart.

"Our planet is on a collision course with a nearby star, Galatin 4. In less than six years both will be destroyed. We are looking for a new home. Earth has a similar atmosphere to Vorgus. In less than twenty-four hours the first spaceships from Vorgus will arrive with reinforcements. After that, many more will come carrying civilians."

"But *we* live here!" Angel replied.

Jesper noticed her tone had softened slightly.

She continued. "We were here first! Humans evolved here thousands of years ago. What gives you the right to take it away from us, to destroy our homes, and to break up our families, in order to save your own?"

"Survival of the species," replied Jesper. "The strongest species have always survived."

Angel got to her feet and stepped toward Jesper. He hissed a warning for her to back off. She complied, shaking slightly.

"Survival of the species is fine for creatures who do not think or feel emotions. But you do. You have just shown me you do," she said, looking into his eyes.

The hatred Jesper had seen earlier had turned to pleading. Now she was trying to survive. She was trying to be the stronger species, and she was succeeding. She had touched his emotions. She had found his weakness—his better judgment. He could not deny that what the Vorgs were doing here was wrong.

He looked at Fly. "I have a son. I can't let myself think that his life might end. You must understand that. I cannot allow my family to give up hope."

Fly looked astounded. "But it's not right to take our lives instead," he said softly.

"We are *not* taking your lives," Jesper shot back. "We are not murderers."

"We're as good as dead when we're desensitized!" shouted Angel. "The Gilded State, huh! Would you consider your son alive if someone turned him into a zombie?"

How could they think him so cruel? "The process can be reversed!" hissed Jesper. "It's not a permanent state! We're only doing this until you come to accept us being here."

Angel didn't move. Fly barely flinched. The silence struck Jesper. What had he said? He had betrayed the Vorgs. His soft heart had allowed him to divulge classified information to the enemy. They had interrogated him, and he had allowed it. He backed out of the room and closed the door quickly, stunned by his own weakness.

He heaved one of the solid tables up against the door angrily. With an enormous growl, he lifted a second table over his head, turned it upside down and allowed it to crash down on the first. That would be sufficient to stop them from leaving. He could not bring himself to use his venom and inflict more pain on the youngsters, but he would not release them. He had to think this through. He had to get out of here for a while.

* * * * *

Targon rubbed his eyes. He and Chip had been sitting in front of the Xandix III for hours. Varl would be delighted with what they had found out and he couldn't wait to see his face.

Someone tapped him on the shoulder. Targon removed the helmet and turned around to see Varl. "How's Matt doing?" he asked his elderly friend.

"Not so good," replied Varl. "He feels very guilty about Angel and Fly not making it back."

"Hope we can get to them in time," said Targon. "I feel sick when I think of them being desensitized."

"We'll find a way," said Varl. "Did you find out anything that could help?"

"Lots," said Targon. "Wait 'til you hear!"

Chip handed Varl his pad of scrawled notes. "We've recorded certain optic clips for you to study."

"I think you'd better read it to me," said Varl, handing the notes back.

Targon grinned. Chip's handwriting was unreadable.

Chip flipped over the first page. "We have a couple of sections showing inside The Factory. Most useful for when we want to free those being held for desensitization."

If The Factory is a Vorg building, how is it that you have the network installed?" asked Varl.

"The only building built by Vorgs is the Great Complex," Chip explained. "The Factory was a privately owned research laboratory before the Vorgs arrived. They took it over and added their own equipment to make it what it is today."

"You can see the materialization chambers, all the exits—and you'll never guess what . . ." Targon said excitedly.

"What?" asked Varl.

"The fire extinguishers haven't been taken down. They're all still on the walls—everywhere you look!"

"The Vorgs didn't remove them?" questioned Varl.

"It appears not," said Chip.

Varl frowned. "Why would they leave them in place after the attack? It makes no sense."

"That's what I thought," said Chip. "So, we monitored Vorg conversations. You can listen to the recordings later. It appears that there is some friction among the upper ranks. Jesper of the Mount, whom you had the misfortune to meet, lost his job as Commander of The

Factory after all the escapes."

Varl laughed. "I bet he's not pleased about that."

Chip smiled. "That's why he was looking for information at the university. Trying to restore his reputation and look good again in the eyes of the Vorg leader."

It makes sense," agreed Varl. "What's the Vorg leader called and what's he like?"

"We know his name is Gubala," Targon answered. "We can't tell you what he's like because he never leaves the Great Complex—the building that the Vorgs built. There's no Xandix III network there, of course."

"What's interesting," Chip continued, "is that Jesper's replacement at The Factory, Harless, seems to be a complete fool. He's not respected by the Vorgs that work for him and he's also out to impress Gubala. There's rivalry between Harless and Jesper that we might be able to turn to our advantage."

Varl rubbed his chin. "All very interesting."

"My guess is that the canisters of Capriclan have been left there to prove a point," continued Chip. "For the same reason, Harless hasn't even ordered that captured humans be restrained."

"That Harless can do a better job at guarding humans than Jesper and that humans pose no real threat," finished Varl.

Chip nodded. "Ironic, really. It's as if Harless is taunting Jesper. Such human qualities found in such ugly beasts."

"I'm sure that there are many similar qualities in all life-forms, no matter how intelligent," said Varl. "Self-preservation for one."

Chip nodded. "We're just about to check the recordings from the Technology Complex again. There might be clues as to where they've taken Angel and Fly."

"Let's go live first and check the recordings later," said Varl.

Chip handed Targon the helmet. "Go to it. We'll begin on the ground floor and work our way up. Start with trimod TC 1 and run through all of the optics linked to that trimod."

Targon liked the Xandix III system. There was no reading or writing involved in operating this computer. He thought about the optic view he needed and stayed focused while Varl looked closely at the huge screen.

"That's the glass door that Matt told me about," said Varl. "Angel probably slipped on all the broken glass."

Targon slowly showed the view through every optic on the ground floor. There was no sign of movement.

"The History Department," announced Chip as Targon changed to trimod TC 47.

"Zoom in on the back of that room," said Varl. "There's a Vorg."

"Try optic 4," said Chip.

Varl sighed. "It's Jesper again."

"What's he doing stacking tables in front of the door?" asked Targon. "Now he's leaving the room."

"There's light coming from under the door. Switch to

optic 5. We should get a view inside the storeroom."

The screen changed. Two figures sat huddled in the corner of the tiny room.

"It's Angel and Fly!" shouted Targon. His heart raced with happiness and excitement. "They don't look as though they've been desensitized."

"That's a surprise," said Chip. "Why do you suppose Jesper didn't take them to The Factory?"

Varl laughed. "After what you've just said? It's my guess that Jesper doesn't want to hand them over to his rival, Harless. Dissension in the ranks of the enemy always works to the opposition's advantage."

"Can we get Angel and Fly out of there?" asked Targon.

"Risky," said Chip. "We don't know where Jesper has gone or for how long."

"Or where the other Vorg is," added Varl. "Matt said there were two in the building."

"So what *can* we do?" asked Targon.

"I'm assuming there's no way of letting them know we can see them?" asked Varl.

Chip shook his head. "None. We'll have to hope they remember the discussions about the Xandix III network."

"For now we carry on as planned," said Varl. "Listen to Angel's conversation with Fly. They may give us something to go on without realizing we're listening in. We'll attempt a rescue during our attack on the Vorgs. I'll go and tell Matt the good news."

* * * *

"I'm proud of you," said Fly.   "You've got guts standing up to that Vorg."

Angel shrugged. "It seems to come naturally. I can't help myself when I get fired up. Don't think it did any good."

"Sure it did," said Fly. "The Vorg shut us in here without using his venom and he's not taken us to be desensitized. Can you believe that stuff about his son?"

Angel fiddled with her hoop earrings. "Until a few moments ago, I thought they were just two-legged, talking, oversized lizards with a craving for power. Now I know better. They can feel what we feel. They've got emotions, and I have to admit, they've got a pretty good reason for being here. If only we could get out of this storeroom and tell the others we're okay."

Fly got up off the floor and gave the door a shove. "Useless.   I heard the Vorg dragging tables.   He's probably stacked them up in front of the door."

"We'll probably die of suffocation or starvation," said Angel sadly. "No one will find us in here."

Fly stood facing the door. He turned quickly around.

"I know that look," said Angel.   "What are you thinking?"

"They might have found us already," said Fly, hardly able to contain himself. "Targon, Chip, Bee and Spider were supposed to be monitoring the Xandix III network, right?"

"Yes!" said Angel, her face brightening. "Do you think they can see us?"

"And hear us. Keep talking. Let's think about everything the Vorg said and repeat it over and over. Hopefully someone will pick up our conversation."

"What did he say that was important?" asked Angel. "Think, come on."

"Desensitization can be reversed. That's great news and important, right?" offered Fly.

"And their planet is doomed. It's going to collide with one of its stars in six years so the Vorgs are looking for a new home." Angel's face dropped. "Oh no! I didn't think about it at the time—I was so angry . . ."

"Didn't think about what?" asked Fly.

"Didn't he say that more Vorg spaceships are arriving in twenty-four hours? We've got to get that message to the others. They've got to get that Earth Defense System working before then."

* * * * *

Targon gasped. Angel had just given him the information they needed. He leaped off the stool, almost knocking Chip over.

"Got to get to Varl. More Vorgs are on their way. Got to get EDS working!" he shouted as he left the room. As he raced toward the kitchen the reality hit. They were nearing the end of Level 3 in Matt's computer game. Would they succeed in freeing the people of Gova? Or would the Vorgs win? He recalled the voice from Matt's computer game. "This is your most dangerous challenge yet. Do you accept the mission?"

It was too late to turn back now, no matter how much the Vorgs terrified him. He, Matt and Varl had made the decision to play Level 3 and had to see the game through to the bitter end. Of one thing he was sure—this would be a battle for survival like no other.

Chapter 18

J esper clutched the map of the coast and a copy of the report he had found in the History Department. He straightened his cloak and strode up the steps of the Great Complex. So much had happened since he last saw Gubala, and yet only forty-eight hours had passed. He hesitated at the entrance, still unsure that he was taking the right course of action. His gut feeling and his conscience told him to do one thing, and yet his loyalty to Gubala prevented him from acting on it.

Jesper materialized outside Gubala's office and exited the chamber. He heard the voices of Yorak and Harless already inside. It was ideal to find them all together. He couldn't wait to see the look on Yorak's face when he divulged the whereabouts of the Resistance base.

Harless puffed out his chest and threw his blue cape over his shoulder as Jesper walked in. "Everything is back under control, sir," Harless said loudly. "It has not been difficult to contain the humans. They are too timid to take action against us."

"You have done well, Harless," Gubala nodded his approval. "I am pleased to hear of no further escapes this week."

"And there have been no sightings of renegade

humans for the past two days," said Yorak. "We have patrolled with vigilence, Great Leader."

Jesper saw disdain in his eyes.

"A good report, Yorak," Gubala hissed.

"Excuse me for interrupting, Great Leader," said Jesper. "I have important information that will be valuable to everyone present."

The folds of skin on Gubala's forehead wrinkled even more as he frowned. "This had better be good, Jesper. You were placed on three days' leave, and you did not book an appointment to see me."

Jesper unrolled the map. "This chart shows the topology of the coast. After witnessing the stolen airbug disappear over the coast yesterday, I researched the rock formations. Caves exist deep within the cliffs."

Gubala placed his stubby arms on the desk. "Did you find the wreckage of the crashed airbug? What is the connection with the caves?"

Jesper swallowed. "I don't think you understand, sir. The airbug mysteriously vanished *into* the cliffs, sir. I believe that the Govan Resistance has a secret base inside."

Yorak began to laugh quietly. Harless smiled, revealing his entire bottom row of teeth. Jesper knew that they were delighting in his discomfort.

Gubala was obviously not amused. "This topographical map shows nothing but the *possibility* of caves. Did you see an entrance for the airbug? How can you support your claim?"

Jesper grunted. "I watched it disappear below the level of the cliff path, sir."

Gubala's face turned to stone. "And you assume that it somehow miraculously went inside the cliffs? Where is your proof?"

"There was no wreckage on the rocks below, and holograms and other computerized methods can disclose an entrance," explained Jesper. "Besides, I used thermal . . ."

Gubala cut him off and bellowed across the table. "These are *humans* we are talking about, not the technological wizards of *our* neighboring planets. Human computer systems are centuries behind our own. Humans have no materialization chambers. Humans know nothing of the workings of the mind and desensitization methods. Humans fly pathetic airbugs, and after centuries of space travel, still cannot make it beyond their own solar system. The Govan Empire and most of planet Earth has made little progress in the last five hundred years!"

Jesper remained silent. He might as well have been talking to a wall. Gubala was not the great leader he had once thought. Gubala was a Vorg who did not wish to see beyond the obvious because it didn't suit his plans to do so. Humans could have technology that Vorgs hadn't yet developed. And most of all, Gubala was not considering the human determination to survive. Jesper had witnessed that strength in the young girl. Humans were like Vorgs. There were those who would do whatever it took to survive and protect their own kind—even if it meant dying for the cause.

"There have been no sightings of renegade humans for the past two days," said Yorak, obviously seizing his opportunity to deal Jesper another blow. "I think that the Resistance is nothing more than an ugly rumor, spread as propaganda by the enemy to waste Vorg resources and energy."

Gubala tapped his claws on his desk. "I couldn't agree more. There is no proof that any significant number of humans have joined together. There has been no evidence of any plot against us, except that one incident at The Factory under your command, Jesper. And you have no proof that the airbug did go into the cliffs. It would take many humans led by a highly organized command to pose any kind of threat to our success."

"But I have other documents . . . " said Jesper, pulling out the research paper on the cliff homes and the thermal imaging data.

Gubala waved his arms wildly and his expression turned to annoyance. "No more of your foolish chatter. I need results, not excuses for incompetence! Tomorrow, large numbers of reinforcements arrive from Vorgus so that we can advance into Javeer. I will not spend time worrying about *what if*—only about *what is*! *What is* certain is that time *is* limited, and so are our resources. If you had shown me undeniable facts and figures that proved the human renegades were more than a handful of troublemakers, I might have considered your opinion."

Jesper stood stunned, hardly able to believe the lack of foresight that he had just witnessed. And this was the leader of the Vorg invasion force?

"You will return to Vorgus for a leave of absence," snapped Gubala.

"Gladly," snarled Jesper. He boiled with rage. "A Vorg that can see no further than the end of his snout, and has nursemaids for officers, should not be in a position of high command."

"How dare you! Your insubordination will cost you your career," hissed Gubala. "Now get out of here before I send *you* to The Factory instead!"

Jesper allowed his tongue to creep to the edge of his jaw and then contained his anger. He was already in enough trouble. Attacking one of his own kind would not be forgiven by any Vorg. He would be placed in a military prison for twenty years. He tipped his spiked head in a gesture of compliance and stalked out of the room.

Jesper was still seething when he returned to the Technology Complex. His presentation to Gubala had been a little thin on facts, but he hadn't been given the chance to show all of his information. Surely his idea had been worthy of consideration. He understood that every leader had to weigh the cost of an operation against the benefits, and that time was critical, but locating and defeating the Resistance was important.

Jesper felt depressed as he laboriously climbed the stairs to the upper level. He missed his family. What had been his purpose here on Earth? He had been judged too quickly for his mistake, he had lost his respect for Gubala, and he believed what Vorgs were doing to humans was wrong.

Jesper hesitated on the top step. Suddenly he knew what he had to do. It was all about survival—his survival and human survival. The girl had shown him that. He had to survive when he returned to Vorgus. He would not allow Gubala, Yorak and Harless to tarnish his reputation. He would stand up for justice, and fight for the rights of humans and honor among Vorgs. His son would be proud—not of his father's achievements in battle, but of his father's values.

Jesper threw open the storeroom door. Angel and Fly looked up at him with bewildered eyes.

"You are free to go," Jesper grunted.

They didn't move.

"Did you not hear? You are free to go."

"Is this a trick to get us to run?" asked Angel.

Jesper snorted. "If I wanted to use my venom on you, I would not need tricks."

Angel got to her feet. "Why are you doing this?"

"Because I am a father. Because I believe in doing what is right. Vorgs have been blinded by their need to survive. Desensitization is wrong, and our survival at the expense of yours is also wrong."

"Thank you . . . thank you so very much," said Angel. "Will you help us?"

"Your fate is out of my hands and in your own. I will

not stand in your way, but I will not help you against my own kind. Nor will I run from my duty as a Vorg commander. I will return to Vorgus as a respected citizen and not as a convict. I do not wish to know your plans or when they will occur. But I will tell you that the Vorg leadership is not respected, and I have a loyal group of supporters who will follow me if Gubala is overthrown. Tell the Resistance to choose their targets wisely. Should you prevail, I will show you how to reverse the desensitization process."

"What do you want in return?" asked Angel.

Jesper smiled. "You are a smart one, girl. I want safe passage back to Vorgus for myself and my comrades."

"Never to return?" asked Angel.

"Never to return," agreed Jesper.

"Done!" said Angel, eagerly squeezing past Jesper.

Fly stood up and took two steps toward the door after her.

"Not you, young man!" Jesper hissed.

Angel turned back, a look of horror on her face. "But you just said we were free to go!"

"*You*, young lady, are free to go. The young man will stay as my insurance. You have my word that I will release him when my safe passage is guaranteed."

"But he's my brother. I can't leave him," said Angel, moving back toward the storeroom.

"Go, Angel. I'll be fine," said Fly, his voice quaking.

Jesper blocked the doorway. "I admire your loyalty,

young lady. It is a good quality. Your brother will not be harmed. Now go—before I change my mind and keep you both."

He closed the storeroom door and walked over to the window, wondering what the next twenty-four hours would bring. "Level Six of the Great Complex would be a good place for the humans to begin their rebellion," he said, as he watched Angel run across the grass toward Main and Bryant.

* * * * *

Varl watched Doc, hard at work. He was hesitant to disturb the man's concentration, but he couldn't contain his curiosity any longer. Boxes full of metal balls, the size of large marbles, covered the tables in Doc's room.

Varl picked up one of the spheres between his thumb and forefinger. He turned it around, looking for some clue as to what it was and how it worked. There were small cracks across the surface.

Doc smiled. "I knew you wouldn't be able to stay away."

"Sorry, but I'm intrigued how you're going to disperse the Capriclan," Varl said. "What are these things?"

"They're old surveillance crabs that I have altered to suit our purpose."

"Crabs? They're spherical!"

Doc smiled. "We had a few crabs already in the cliff homes. Snake came back with plenty more from the technology labs. The technology is pretty old compared to the Xandix system." He picked up a trimod. "What's the number on the side of that one?"

Varl turned the sphere around slowly until he saw the small black numbers. He squinted. "It says fifty-nine."

Doc pressed fifty-nine on the trimod. There was a shrill mechanical sound. The ball vibrated and pinched Varl's hand. He screamed and dropped it to the floor. It sprouted ten legs and scuttled in a crab-like manner sideways across the room. Doc was obviously amused at the shock he had given Varl. He roared with laughter.

"You didn't tell me it had pincers," Varl laughed with him. "Sorry, but I couldn't resist."

"How will these work?" asked Varl.

"Each pressurized sphere will contain enough Capriclan to cause at least temporary blindness to all the occupants of an average-sized room. They are computerized so that we can control their direction and the time they release the chemical. We can drop them into ventilation shafts in each of the target buildings and guide them to the desired place."

Varl nodded. "I'm impressed."

"While you sort out the Earth Defense System with Matt, these little creatures will have the Vorg population under control."

Targon peered around the corner. "I hope there are no more of these things crawling about," he said, holding up the crab.

Doc shook his head. "All clear. That was my

demonstration model."

"Have you heard the latest news?" asked Targon.

Varl nodded. "Snake's gone to meet Angel. We're very relieved they're both okay, and that at least *she* is coming back."

"I hope we're going to use the information Jesper of the Mount gave us," said Targon, eagerly fingering the crabs on the table.

"What exactly are you referring to?" asked Doc.

Targon chattered excitedly. "Jesper suggested to Angel that we target the Vorg leadership."

"But we have no blueprints of the Great Complex. It would be hard to know where to start," said Doc.

Targon grinned. "This is the best part. After Angel had gone, Jesper said something we can use. He didn't know about the Xandix III optics in the room, of course."

"Well . . ." said Doc. "What did he say?"

"He said that Level Six would be a good place to start the rebellion."

Doc's eyes lit up. "Really? Well, that *is* useful. Chip scanned the complex using trimods in the street opposite, and made a guess that there were no more than six levels. That makes it easy. Gubala and his leaders are probably on the top floor."

"That's what Chip said. But how will we get these crabs into the air vents on the sixth level?" asked Targon.

"Easy," said Varl. "Assuming Angel is in a fit state when she gets back."

Targon wrinkled his nose. "I don't get it."

Varl put his arm around Targon's shoulders. "You and Angel will deliver them personally."

"You're joking, right?" shouted Targon.

"Never more serious, my boy. We'll use the airbug and land on the roof. Vorgs build square, flat, ugly structures. The design of the Great Complex is ideal for our purpose."

"Hmm," said Doc. "We can't guarantee it, but I'd lay bets that there are air vents on the roof."

Targon groaned. "I don't believe it! You want Angel and me to risk our lives based on the chance that there are vents on the roof? I've heard you tell Matt so many times that you are a scientist and don't gamble with odds!"

"You seem to be doing that a lot lately, Varl," said Matt, joining the conversation. He entered Doc's room and picked up one of the crabs.

Varl winked. "But you keep telling me this is all a game, my boy."

"It's hardly that!" snapped Doc. "We're fighting for our survival here. Sometimes risks have to be taken, and this is one of them."

"Don't worry," Matt said in a reassuring tone. "We're taking the Vorgs very seriously."

Can you be ready with the crabs in a couple of hours, Doc?" asked Varl.

"If you leave me in peace and quiet to get these things loaded," he replied.

"We're already out of here," said Matt, dragging Varl

and Targon through the door and into the tunnel.

Varl lowered his voice. "Glad to see that you've perked up, Matt, my boy."

"Now that Angel's coming back, and Fly is safe for the moment, I feel a lot better, thanks."

"Good. We've a long night ahead and a lot to do. Targon, you'll go with Angel to disperse a dozen Capriclan crabs in the Great Complex and then act as backup for us. Other members of the Resistance will take the remaining crabs to various locations around Bay City. Matt, you will accompany Snake and me to the spaceport."

"It's not going to be an easy mission, is it?" Matt asked.

Varl shook his head.

Matt grimaced. "Did you come up with a backup plan?"

"Of sorts," said Varl. "I've been working on it with Chip. Ordinary weapons only maim Vorgs, and Vorgs can regenerate body parts if they're not too badly injured. Explosives—even if we could get our hands on enough in time—could kill as many humans as Vorgs. We can't forget that wherever there are Vorgs in Bay City, there are also desensitized humans. That's the beauty of Capriclan. The Vorgs will be in temporary pain and blinded while humans are unaffected by the chemical."

"But even if they're blind, the Vorgs won't lose the use of their venom. Their tongues can still lash out at us," Matt pointed out.

"Blindness and pain will confuse and disorient them. Their tongues *will* lash out as a natural defense, I'm sure," said Varl. "Chip is putting electrical stunners on long poles, which the Resistance can use to keep the blind Vorgs at a distance while we herd them into secure areas. Then we'll have to find a way to get rid of them from Gova permanently."

Targon sighed and shook his head. "That's the backup plan?" He turned to Matt. "When your computer warned that this was the most difficult level of *Keeper of the Kingdom*, that was no joke. I just hope we can beat Level 3 and all get home again."

"Home," Matt lamented. "I got so caught up in all the drama, I had almost forgotten what we were here to do."

"It's easy to forget that we're not part of this empire," said Varl. "We've made so many new friends. Now we must concentrate on the game and what we're expected to do."

"Activate the Keeper and free the people," whispered Targon.

Varl smiled. "I'm glad that you've got that straight. Just remember that when you're on the roof of the Great Complex!"

Targon shuddered. "I'll be fine. There won't be any Vorgs up there."

Varl pursed his lips and decided not to respond to Targon's comment. With materialization, Vorgs could appear at any time. He turned to Matt. "I suggest you familiarize yourself with Chip's updated EDS program.

There's a lot you'll need to know in a short space of time."

"Just get me inside the control room," replied Matt. "I'll do the rest."

"Okay, let's get to it," said Varl, looking at his watch. "Angel will be back soon, and Doc should be finished in another hour. All teams will go under the cover of darkness at eleven."

Varl watched Matt and Targon head off down the tunnels in opposite directions. It was going to be a long night.

Chapter 19

Even in the dark, the imposing octagonal structure of spaceport control was enough to make anyone silent. It was four stories high with a three-story concrete base and huge glass angular windows enclosing the control room on the top level.

Matt forgot his nervousness. He stared at the bright lights that illuminated the enormous landing pad and surrounding field. There were no trees and no other buildings near the control tower. How would they get under the perimeter fence and run across the field to the tower without being seen?

Matt lay on his stomach. The ground was hard. He scratched his nose, forgetting that Varl had painted their faces with black grease. Now his hand was also black. He rubbed it on the grass. He felt like a commando on a night raid. Spider had insisted that they all wear dark clothing, and he had laughed at her attention to detail. Now he was grateful.

It was midnight. They had just emerged from the sewers. Matt waited apprehensively for Snake to give the word to move out. He hoped it would be soon—the pack on his back was heavy. Varl had divided the equipment between the three of them, and yet Matt still seemed to be carrying an enormous weight.

The Xandix helmet on his head was cumbersome. Chip had reconfigured one of the helmets with a transmitter and a receiver. The network would pick up Matt's thoughts and type them on the screen back in the computer room. Chip would know what Matt was doing and be able to relay information back to him through a small receiver in the helmet. Across the front of the helmet was a visor, which acted as binoculars with night vision. It was clever, but heavy to wear.

"Let's go to the perimeter fence," said Varl. "Stay low and don't touch—it's electrified."

Snake slithered along on his belly like it was something he did regularly. Matt followed awkwardly. Without thinking, he reached for the fence to pull himself closer.

"Don't touch!" snapped Varl.

Matt quickly pulled back his fingers.

"The fence is electrified," Varl repeated.

Matt shuddered. He had nearly fried his brains without the help of the Vorgs.

Varl undid his pack and took out a few simple tools. "Chip has given me clips that will deactivate the fence between these two posts. The moment I've cut the wire, we can go through." He placed clips at various points along the fence and began to cut the thin mesh.

"Good thing them Vorgs 'aven't been 'ere long enough to change the old fence to something stronger," said Snake.

"They *have* been here long enough," muttered Varl

as he worked. "But they don't consider us any real threat if we do break through." He laughed. "They'll realize their mistake once we're done tonight."

"Are you ready?" whispered Snake.

"Not yet," said Varl, wielding the large rubber-handled cutters. "See anything, Matt?"

Matt stared through the helmet visor. "Stay down. I see the lights of an airbug. It's coming in low."

"That has to be the new shift of Vorg controllers, right on time," said Varl with satisfaction. "The controller shuttles are the only airbugs allowed near the spaceport. Chip's done a good job finding out information with Xandix III."

"It's landed. The back is opening," reported Matt.

"How many Vorgs?" Snake asked.

"Three," replied Matt.

Snake sighed. He looked at Varl anxiously. "'urry it up, mate, or it'll be too late to run during their shift change."

Matt watched Varl cutting through the wire. The older man twisted his face, in a way that Matt had come to recognize as meaning trouble.

"This last piece *won't* break," grunted Varl. "My aging fingers are giving me a hard time."

"'Ere," said Snake. "I'll try." He pursed his lips and struggled with the cutters until the wire mesh snapped.

"Great going, Snake," said Varl, putting the equipment back in his pack.

"The Vorgs are approaching the base of spaceport

control," Matt announced.

"You both ready?" asked Varl. "We'll wait for them to take the elevator up to the control room. Then we'll run as far as the landing pad. Hide behind the first spotlight. The structure is plenty big enough. If we stay in its shadow, they won't see us from the control room."

"The doors have closed. They're on their way," said Matt.

Varl bent the mesh back. "Okay, we're going!"

Snake pushed his pack through first, and was up and running before Matt had registered that they were off.

"Go, Matt," said Varl, urging him through the opening.

Matt ran after Snake. He dared not look anywhere but ahead. He dived behind the drum-shaped light and curled up to make room for Varl.

The old man threw himself on the ground, panting heavily. "My sprinting days are done."

"Now what?" asked Matt. His adrenaline had kicked in, and his heart raced.

"We wait for the previous shift of Vorgs to come down from the control room," panted Varl. "They should leave in the same airbug. Once they're gone, we'll run for the elevator."

"Won't the Vorgs in the control room see us?" asked Matt.

"It's a chance we'll have to take," said Varl. "Chip listened to some of the control room talk through the Xandix III network. He thinks the new shift will be making equipment checks for the first fifteen minutes."

Matt watched the elevator doors open. "Here's the outgoing shift." Three Vorgs exited the elevator and lumbered up to the airbug, talking and grunting. They clambered in and the vehicle took off. "Okay, all clear."

"Let's go," whispered Varl.

Matt bounded across the tarmac toward the elevators after the others. There was a loud clunk. A bright searchlight on the roof suddenly illuminated a large area close to the building. It began sweeping directly in front of the landing pad. Matt dropped to the ground in panic, hoping that his dark clothes and blackened face would blend with the tarmac. He gulped. Any movement would be seen. He was stuck.

Matt waited for the light to move over him and then lifted his head slightly. He could just see Varl and Snake in the shadows by the elevator. He was holding them up. He couldn't stay where he was. What could he do? He had to risk it and run. He counted the seconds that it took for the light to pass over him and then return. Twenty-five exactly. He counted a second time to make sure. Could he make it to the building in twenty-five seconds? It would be close, but he had no choice.

He waited for the light to pass over him again, sprang to his feet and took off. 1–2-3 . . . He was racing for his life . . . 7–8-9 . . . He didn't know he could run so fast . . . 11-12-13 . . . Pains shot down his legs . . . 16-17-18 . . . Varl's hand was outstretched . . . 20-21-22 . . . Was he going to make it? A second to go . . . Matt dived into the shadows at Snake's feet, clutching his chest and gulping for air, just as the light flickered on his heels.

Varl patted him on the back. "Well done, my boy. That took guts. Sorry we can't give you time to recover, but every second we stay here we're putting ourselves at risk."

Matt nodded, gasping. "Understood. Let's go." Snake helped him up.

"Capriclan ready?" asked Varl.

"Ready," said Snake, removing two crabs from his pack.

"One should do it," said Varl. "Let's save the rest for when we need them." The elevator doors opened. "Matt, ask Chip if he can see the Vorgs in the control room through the Xandix network."

"Affirmative," said Matt. The sound of Chip's voice coming through his helmet was reassuring. "Two Vorgs are running checks on the computer system. The third is operating the searchlight. All three Vorgs have their backs to the elevator."

Varl removed the telescopic electric rod from his pack. "Better be ready for them. Get out the trimod, Matt. You'll need to activate the crab the moment the elevator doors open."

The ride up to the control room seemed to take forever. The anticipation grew. Matt's palms sweated. He hoped he'd be able to punch in the number on the trimod fast enough. The elevator reached the top. A buzzer sounded! The Vorgs had a warning system. Varl looked horror-struck. This they had not anticipated.

There would be no surprise entry.

"Chip says the Vorgs are walking to the elevator," said Matt in panic.

"Get ready," said Varl as the doors opened. "Activate the crab!"Matt keyed in 23 on the trimod. Doc's Capriclan was about to be put to its first test.

* * * * *

Angel turned off the airbug lights and relied on the computer navigation system to fly them to the Great Complex. There was nothing she could do to reduce the noise of the engines. She hoped they had timed it right. The Resistance should have begun their attacks all around the city. In the confusion that would follow an airbug landing on the roof might not be noticed.

They approached the outer city limits. The sky was quiet.

"Something's wrong," said Targon. "There should be lights and airbugs everywhere by now."

Angel felt sick. Couldn't anything go right just once? "Perhaps the Capriclan didn't work," she said, hardly daring to say it out loud."

"That was my thought," muttered Targon. "You'll have to go back over the coast and circle again. We're coming in too close. You'll be heard, and we'll have airbugs on our tail."

"Turning now."

"Wait!" shouted Targon. "Look over there. That

whole street's lit up. Something's happening."

"I see airbugs heading that way," said Angel.

"The Resistance must be attacking!" shouted Targon. "Look—the whole eastern edge of Bay City is illuminated."

Angel gritted her teeth. "Then it's happening, and now it's our turn. Look for the Great Complex. You should recognize it from viewing the street optics."

"There, that's definitely it," said Targon, pointing through the windshield.

There was no mistaking the ugly monstrosity in the distance. The concrete square stood out amongst the elegant glass buildings built by the Govans. Angel set her sights on a large white X on the roof, which marked a landing pad.

More airbugs appeared in the night sky. The lights flickered as they swooped in to set down on the streets and let out Vorg reinforcements.

"I hope Doc made enough Capriclan," said Targon.

"Only time will tell," said Angel, pulling back on the wheel. "I'm going in for a landing."

Targon nodded. "Go for it."

She lowered the bug. "There's a strong wind. It's not going to be easy."

"You can do it," Targon urged.

"Drat! There's a materialization chamber on the roof."

Targon shuddered. "That means we could run into Vorgs."

"Don't worry—I'll keep watch. Can you see all four

air vents?"

"One in each corner, I think. Start with the far one. If you can get close enough, I may be able to drop the crabs inside without getting out."

Angel fought against the wind. She had trouble keeping the bug steady. Targon leaned out the open side and stretched his arm over the first vent. Just as he opened his fist to release the crab, the airbug was blown sideways by a gust. Targon was jolted to the left. He dropped the crab on the roof.

"Zang it! I missed!" said Targon. "It's too windy. I'll have to get out and do it by hand."

"Hang on, I'm landing," said Angel, putting down on the white X in the center of the rooftop. "Be careful," she shouted as Targon leaped from the cockpit.

She watched Targon pick up the crab he had dropped and throw it down the vent. He dug inside his pack for a second crab, punched in the codes on the trimod, and pelted across to the next vent.

"So far, so good," said Angel. Her eyes focused on the materialization chamber. There was definitely a surveillance system of some kind on the top of it. Vorgs would be on their way. "Keep going, Targon. Two down, two to go."

Targon raced to the other corner and released more crabs into the vent, then made his way to the last.

Angel turned just in time to see two Vorgs materialize. They were armed with jazooks. "Watch out, Targon!" she screamed. But he didn't respond. Angel realized that he couldn't hear her warnings above the noise of the wind and the airbug.

The Vorgs exited the chamber and began firing at her. Angel lifted the airbug into the air and scooted sideways over the edge of the building. She couldn't risk the bug taking a hit.

Targon had seen the Vorgs. He began to run toward the airbug hovering at the edge of the building. Angel struggled to keep the vehicle steady and level with the rooftop. Would he have the guts to jump?

The Vorgs were closing in. Any second, their jazooks would be in range. There was a gap of two feet between the bug and the edge. She couldn't risk going in any closer. Could he do it? Her heart pounded as she tried to keep the airbug steady. Just two seconds more . . .

Targon ran at top speed. He leaped off the rooftop and threw himself head first into the bug, knocking Angel sideways and pushing her hands off the wheel. The bug began to plummet. Angel grabbed for the controls.

"Hold on!" she shouted, pulling back on the wheel.

Targon struggled to sit. Angel leveled the bug and it began to climb back up the side of the building. Angel looked in horror out of the windshield. The Vorgs were aiming at them. She hadn't gained enough speed to pull away.

"Throw a crab!" she shouted.

Targon hurled one onto the roof and set the trimod. The crab exploded at the Vorgs' feet, releasing a purple mist. The Vorgs fired their jazooks randomly as they staggered about, hissing and howling. Shots rang out inside the bug. The windshield smashed.

Targon screamed, "I'm hit! I'm hit!"

Angel swept the airbug into the air and away from the Great Complex.

"Are you okay? Where'd they get you?" she gasped.

"My shoulder," mumbled Targon. His eyes began to roll.

Angel looked across at him. There was blood everywhere. His clothes were soaked. The seat was a mess. His injury looked serious.

"Hang in there," said Angel. She choked back the tears. She had to stay focused. She had to get him back to the base or he might die.

"It hurts bad," Targon whimpered.

She tried to joke with him. "You did great . . . for a boy,"

Targon could barely manage to smile. "Get me . . . back . . . please," he stammered.

"Just hang on. Doc will fix you up in no time."

Targon didn't reply. His eyes were shut and his body was slumped to one side. Angel gulped. This was not the happy ending she had envisioned.

Chapter 20

A lashing tongue shot through the gap in the opening elevator doors. Matt jumped to one side, giving Snake a clear shot with the crab.

The Vorgs looked down at the strange object that crawled sideways across the floor. It exploded with an unthreatening snap. The purple mist shot into the room. The squealing and hissing that followed was a sure sign that Doc's Capriclan had done its job. The Vorgs tried to cover their eyes. They staggered blindly in every direction, tongues lashing and striking out at anything in their paths.

Varl extended the electric rod to its full length. He prodded the Vorgs one after another, forcing them to move away from the elevator doors. "Get to work, Matt, my boy! Snake, help me get these brutes into the emergency bunker. It's a concrete-reinforced room in the center of the building. It'll keep them out of our way while we work."

Matt brushed past Varl and walked up to the enormous semi-circular console. He stood dazed by thousands of flickering lights. This was a far cry from any computer system he had ever seen. Although Chip had warned him about its complexity, he was still shocked. He tried to block out the hissing and growling coming from the Vorgs behind him and concentrate on his task. Matt ran his hands lightly over the numerous controls. There were no keyboards and yet no helmets to put on, either. He didn't know where to begin. *Chip? I hope you're there. This is not what I had expected.*

Matt listened to Chip's instructions through the helmet.

"The control room computers were developed twenty years ago," Chip explained. "It's such a complex system, we hadn't got around to converting it over to Xandix III before the Vorgs arrived. Find the screenball."

"Screenball," repeated Matt. He picked up a small green ball from a tray in the console. It was a device vaguely like the mouse he used at home, except that it rolled freely under the palm of his hand. He did as Chip instructed and soon brought up a comprehensive menu. He needed to open both the Epsilon System and somehow locate the route taken by arriving Vorg spaceships. *I can't see any Epsilon System in the program files.*

"Search for Earth Defense System in the data base," Chip replied.

Matt was amazed. Chip was answering his thoughts as quickly as they entered his head. The Xandix III was incredible.

"Yes, it's an amazing system," agreed Chip.

Matt smiled. He'd better control what he was thinking!

"Have you found EDS?" asked Chip.

No," replied Matt, already feeling frustrated.

"Try Epsilon Earth Defense System," suggested Chip.

EESD, thought Matt. *This has to be it. The computer won't let me into the data base. It says I need a security red passcode.*

"Enter chip417_groupd/techsupp. My code should still be active for our old files. I doubt the Vorgs have changed them. They need the control room system as backup navigation for their spaceships."

Matt typed in the code. Here goes. Something's happening.

Varl sat down in the chair next to him. "Any luck, my boy?"

"We've managed to pull up the Epsilon files—but we knew that would be the easy part with Chip helping," replied Matt. He scrolled down the menu. *What am I looking for, Chip?*

"You need to find the program that controls Epsilon EDS activation."

Okay. That was easy, found it. Now what?

"Now it gets complicated," said Chip. His voice took on a serious tone. "How good are you at hacking?"

"I'm not," replied Matt out loud.

"Not what?" asked Varl.

"Chip asked if I was good at computer hacking."

"Oh." Varl picked up another green screenball from the tray. "What do we have to do?"

Matt paused as he listened to Chip's instructions.

"We have to pull up the recent Vorg activity and track the last couple of spaceships that arrived," Matt repeated.

"Shouldn't be too difficult," said Varl. "Even if the Vorgs didn't keep a travel log, the information will be stored somewhere in the memory banks."

"Not difficult—just very time-consuming. The memory banks on a computer like this will be huge."

"And that's time we don't have," said Varl. "There has to be a better way. Do we know anything about the journeys of Vorg spaceships?"

"I saw one spaceship arrive when I was in the cornfield. The noise was incredible and the size of it . . . quite amazing."

"When was that?" asked Varl.

"The day we arrived," replied Matt. "I was talking to Targon about UFOs. Let me see . . . I also met Angel that night. That would make it the afternoon of June 8, 2540."

"Now we're getting somewhere," said Varl with enthusiasm.

"I'll key in that date as a search mechanism," said Matt. "Zang it! That was fast. Here's the data already. Chip says to try and backtrack, and see if we can plot the journey the spaceship took from Vorgus."

"Bring up the galaxy map on the main screen," said Varl, pointing to a huge monitor in the center of the room.

"Look at that!" said Matt, as the constellations and planets appeared. "Vorgus is light years away from our solar system."

"That's a whole different kind of space travel from what we know," said Varl. "I can only begin to imagine . . ."

"Okay, the information's all there. Chip says to open the cosmic locator."

"Cosmic locator opened," said Varl. "Ask him to give us the necessary equation."

"Okay," said Matt, typing in a long list of letters and numbers. "Based on the previous routes of the Vorgs' spaceships, the computer should work out the coordinates to program into Epsilon for defending Earth."

"It's thinking."

"Could take a few minutes," said Matt.

"Well, so far, so good," said Varl, relaxing in his chair. "We'll just have to be patient."

"You don't 'ave time," said Snake, running up to the console. "There's another airbug outside. Them Vorgs will be up 'ere in seconds."

"Got some Capriclan ready?" asked Varl. "We'll have to try and hold them off long enough to reprogram EDS. Stay with it, Matt. I'm going with Snake to meet the elevator."

The buzzer sounded. Matt looked over his shoulder to see Varl positioned with the electric rod and Snake poised to throw a crab.

The elevator doors opened. The thick wrinkled skin of a Vorg was instantly visible inside. Varl stabbed at the creature through the widening gap. The Vorg hissed in pain.

"Stop! It's me. It's Fly. It's okay. Put down the Capriclan."

The doors were now fully open. Varl and Snake didn't move. Matt left the console in disbelief. They all stared at the sight. Fly and Jesper of the Mount stood side by side, the Vorg towering above the young man. Jesper raised his claws in the air as if in surrender. His tongue remained inside his jaw, and he made no threatening gestures.

Varl hesitated for a moment and then pulled back his rod. Snake slowly lowered his arm, but still maintained a firm grip on the crab.

"Fly, what's going on?" asked Matt.

"The rebellion is at a stalemate," said Fly.

"What happened?" asked Varl.

"Your Resistance forces overcame my comrades where they had the element of surprise in their favor," said Jesper of the Mount. "Many Vorgs are now blind, and many of your people died from jazook wounds or strong doses of venom."

"Then you've come to ask us to surrender?" asked Matt.

Jesper laughed through his teeth. "Indeed not. Didn't the girl, Angel, tell you about my position?"

"We had heard that you wanted safe passage to Vorgus in return for showing us how to reverse desensitization," said Varl, "but it's not easy to believe—especially when I barely escaped the atrocities at The Factory under *your* command."

Jesper bowed his head. "I am truly sorry for that. I knew we had met before."

"I don't understand. Why are you here?" pressed Matt. "Are you joining forces with us?"

Jesper laughed again. "I will not take up arms against my own kind. However, most of the city is under the control of your Resistance and only one Vorg stronghold remains."

"The Factory," Matt guessed immediately.

"Correct—The Factory," repeated Jesper. "Gubala was not in the Great Complex when your people attacked. He went to see Harless at The Factory when the first trouble in Bay City was reported. They are pressing Vorgs to continue to fight. Humans are being held hostage. I am here in an attempt to prevent further injury on both sides. We could continue to fight each other until Bay City is wiped out of humans, and the majority of Vorgs are blind. What good will that do any of us?"

"I don't understand," said Varl. "You won't take up arms against your own kind and yet you seem to be on our side."

Jesper nodded. A toothy smile crept across his jaw. "A fair evaluation of my position. I believe that this can be solved by negotiation."

"Aren't you thinking of your own position?" asked Varl. "We know that you were treated badly by Gubala and Harless. Aren't you really here because you want revenge?"

Jesper looked shocked by this accusation. His brow furrowed into deep folds of skin. "You know a lot. I'm not sure why I'm surprised. I told Gubala that we had underestimated you."

"We want the truth," pushed Matt. He looked straight into Jesper's yellow eyes. "Tell us the truth."

"Another youngster with such bravado and determination," said Jesper. "Yes, I did set out for revenge. I wanted to bring you all down so that I looked good in the eyes of Gubala. I'm bitter for the way in which I have been treated. I can't deny that. However, I'm being honest when I tell you that is no longer my intention. I wish to make up for all that has been done to you. I wish to return home to Vorgus with my head held high and with my integrity intact."

Varl stood silently, staring at the Vorg. Snake frowned as if he were trying to weigh up the situation. Matt wondered if a Vorg were capable of feeling remorse. He looked at Fly for his answer. "Do you believe him?"

Fly nodded. "He let Angel go, and he brought me here. He had no reason to treat us kindly. Jesper *will* show us how to reverse desensitization."

Varl folded his hands across his stomach and said, "What do you propose we do to end this stalemate?"

"We go to The Factory together," said Jesper. "I have loyal Vorgs there who I am sure can be persuaded to follow me if you guarantee . . ." He broke off in mid-sentence.

Matt followed Jesper's eyes to the huge screen in the

center of the room. In red letters were the words *Epsilon EDS activated.*

"What have you activated?" asked Jesper.

"Epsilon Earth Defense System," said Varl. "Any further spaceships that enter our atmosphere will be treated as enemy craft and shot down with lasers."

"I can see that you will fight to the end," said Jesper. His voice conveyed a mixture of sadness and desperation.

"What do you want us to do?" shouted Snake. "Let more of you Vorgs settle 'ere?"

"Do I have your guarantee that if we return to Vorgus, you will not use your defense system on spaceships leaving your atmosphere?"

Varl nodded. "We intend to protect our planet, not destroy your species."

Jesper stepped back into the elevator. "Then I suggest we resolve this situation quickly. The next Vorg spaceship is due to enter your atmosphere in less than six hours. Time is short."

* * * * *

Matt felt strange sitting in an airbug with a Vorg, after all they had been through. Jesper landed the vehicle outside the main entrance to The Factory. A contingent of guards carrying jazooks stood outside. Their leathery faces looked confused as Matt, Varl, Snake, and Fly followed Jesper up to the entrance.

"We are here to see Gubala," explained Jesper.

One of the guards thrust his jazook at Jesper. Jesper turned his head and hissed at him, his tongue poised to lash out. The guard quickly recoiled and lowered his weapon.

"Wise decision," snapped Jesper.

Urg met them in the corridor. Matt instantly saw that this Vorg was pleased to see Jesper, but he also seemed confused.

"So you found the Resistance," said Urg. He eyed Matt and the others with suspicion.

"Not exactly," replied Jesper.

"Are you handing them over to Gubala and Harless for desensitization?"

Every bone in Matt's body prickled. He felt hot and then cold. What had they done by placing their trust in one of these brutes? Jesper had charmed them with his language and eloquent talk of good intentions. Now the four of them had stupidly walked into a den of Vorgs with little protection. He looked at Varl. It was obvious by the expression on Varl's face that he was thinking the same thing.

Jesper leaned close to Urg. "Do you trust me?" he hissed.

Urg bowed his huge head. "You have my complete loyalty, as always."

"Then lead us to Gubala. Round up my supporters and meet me upstairs in the desensitization chamber."

Panic rushed over Matt as he walked down the

corridor. Memories of his escape with Angel came flooding back. Had Jesper tricked them into leaving the spaceport and coming here? He would probably use their capture to secure his reinstatement as a Vorg commander. In six hours the Vorgs could easily work out how to shut down Epsilon EDS—the system had been simple enough to activate. Jesper would be a hero.

How could they escape once they were upstairs, headed for the desensitization chamber? Four of them couldn't fight off several dozen Vorgs. The fire extinguishers were still on the walls. Matt eyed the canisters. Should he seize the opportunity? How long should they continue to trust Jesper? Snake had removed his backpack and was carrying it. Matt could see his hand nervously dipping inside. Even Fly, who had been so trusting in the control room, now looked terrified.

Jesper opened the door to the chamber. Matt looked along the walls as he stepped inside. There were only two Capriclan canisters—one on each side of the door. It would be enough in an emergency to get them out of the room. But then what? The place was swarming with Vorgs.

Gubala stood by the windows on the opposite wall. He was taller than most Vorgs and looked dignified in a rich golden cloak. Harless stood alongside him, chest puffed out. The look on his face changed from pride to anger when Jesper entered the room.

Matt hovered near the door close to one canister.

Snake clutched his pack to his chest. Fly, seemingly sensing Matt's intentions, moved next to the other canister. Varl walked bravely forward with Jesper.

"I'm pleased to see that you have redeemed yourself," said Gubala, placing his thick arm around Jesper's shoulder in a gesture of comradeship. "With the capture of the Resistance leaders, the other renegade humans will stop the rebellion. You have done well." The folds of skin hanging beneath Gubala's jaw wobbled as he laughed.

Matt felt movement behind him. At least thirty Vorgs filed into the room, blocking the exit. Matt felt faint. His game had warned that Level 3 would be the most difficult. Had they played carefully and come so far, only to be defeated at the end by their willingness to trust Jesper? It was human nature to look for the good in everyone. Jesper had seemed sincere. Matt had desperately wanted to believe that a monster like Jesper could have a heart, but placing his trust in the enemy might have cost him the game—and perhaps also his life.

Jesper threw off Gubala's arm and hissed loudly. "You fool!" he bellowed. "You did not see the Resistance as a threat. You did not want to listen when I told you that all the signs of a rebellion were there. You were too determined to continue with the invasion."

Harless of the Waters cowered noticeably.

Gubala backed away, placing himself between Harless and a Vorg armed with a jazook. "I was hasty in my judgment of you, I admit. To make up for my oversight, you will be given the position of Intelligence Leader for the Invasion Force. The other commanders will report to you."Matt gulped. Was this what Jesper was waiting for? He inched close to the Capriclan canister.

"Oversight?" bellowed Jesper. He hissed again. "I do not want your concocted position of Intelligence Leader! I once had great respect for you, Gubala, but no longer. Your interest in this invasion has only been self-serving. You do not really care about the Vorg race—only about your prestige as a conquering Vorg leader."

"And where has your softness for the humans got you, Jesper?" sneered Harless. "You will return to Vorgus, not as a savior of our species, but with hundreds of Vorgs who are blind. A defeat at the hands of an inferior race will be looked upon with shame and dishonor. How will your son be able to look you in the face?"

"Easily!" said Jesper. He walked toward Harless and stared him in the eyes. "What we have done to humans in this desensitization chamber is inexcusable. My son will know that I stand for honor, for compassion and for integrity. What will your son be able to say about you?"

"That I stood by Gubala!" Harless spat.

"Then stand by him!" replied Jesper. He turned and addressed the armed Vorgs. "The humans have set powerful lasers to attack all incoming Vorg spaceships. I have been guaranteed safe passage home. Who is returning with me?"

Matt was speechless. His instinct to trust this huge brute had been correct after all. He waited for a cheer of approval, but none followed. A hush fell over the room. Gubala's face twisted into a smile. Harless laughed, his belly shaking. Then one by one the Vorgs threw their jazooks to the floor.

Harless quit laughing. He looked at the row of angry Vorgs, he looked at Gubala, and then he looked at Matt. His eyes narrowed. He lunged for a jazook. Jesper pounced on top of him. There was snarling, hissing and squealing. Claws struck out at flesh, and spikes grated on the floor as they struggled for control of the weapon. Matt watched as the huge lizards rolled first one way and then the other, legs and arms striking out, tongues lashing.

There was a loud blast from the jazook. Matt gasped in horror. The room was silent again.

Finally, Jesper rolled over on to his back, his chest rising and falling quickly. Harless remained on the floor in a pool of blood, a dozen arrows protruding from his stomach and neck. Gubala seemed to wither as he stared at Harless of the Waters' lifeless body.

Fly ran forward and extended his hand to Jesper. Matt watched in amazement as Jesper muttered his thanks and staggered to his feet. The Vorg victor draped his bleeding arm across Fly's shoulder as he regained his breath.

"I assume you are stripping me of my command and taking over?" said Gubala soberly.

Jesper laughed. "You still don't understand, do you? This is not about power! I will not mutiny against my own kind! I do not wish to become the Vorg leader unless I am rightfully given that position. I will follow *you*, Gubala. I will follow you on another quest—a quest that respects the rights of all living beings and a quest that finds us another planet to inhabit. And perhaps I will regain my respect for you as a fair and just leader on that journey."

Gubala stared at Jesper with narrowed eyes, as if he couldn't quite believe what he had just heard. "I did what I did to save Vorgs from extinction," he said, attempting to defend his actions.

"But Vorgs are not murderers," said Jesper. "We must save our species, but not at the expense of another."

"I hope that I can live up to the trust you have just placed in me," Gubala said quietly.

"You will," said Jesper with confidence. "I hope everyone in this room has learned an important lesson today. In spite of our desperate situation, we must not lose sight of who we are. Vorgs should never be feared by another kind."

* * * * *

Matt watched with relief as the last Vorg trudged up the ramp into the enormous spacecraft. The ramp lifted and the door lowered. It reminded him of a scene from a television movie he had once seen. Varl had temporarily turned off Epsilon Earth Defense System to allow the Vorgs to leave safely.

"Good luck, Jesper of the Mount," whispered Matt.

"Good riddance!" corrected Angel.

"We did see his good side in the end," said Matt. "*And* he showed us how to reverse the desensitization process."

Angel shuddered. "That smell of burning is something that will stay with me the rest of my life. Let us hope that no Govan has been left with permanent damage. How's Targon doing?"

"Much better, thanks to you. We'll be leaving in a day or two. He told me how you saved his life."

Angel blushed. "I'm just a great pilot! Want a ride back?"

Matt laughed. "If it's a choice between going with you or taking the sewers with Snake, you've got my vote!"

* * * * *

Matt sat on Varl's bed, clutching his laptop.

"We did it, my boy," said Varl.

Matt nodded. "It was close, for a while."

Varl laughed. "I must admit, I first thought how stupid we had been to trust Jesper."

"If there's one thing I've learned while playing all three levels of my game, it's that no species is *all* bad. There's always plenty of good to find." Matt opened his laptop.

"Be sure to remember that when you return to USA 2010," laughed Varl.

Targon entered the room, his arm in a sling. "I don't know about including cybergons in that assessment. I think they're *all* out to destroy humanity."

Matt smiled and moved along the bed to make room for Targon. "But of course. Have you forgotten Protector 101 from your home of Zaul? Without his help we might never have completed Level 1 of my game! How's the arm?"

"Sore, but I'll live. Doc said I was really lucky."

Matt opened *Keeper of the Kingdom*.

"So this is really the end of the game?" asked Varl.

"Does that mean you finally accept that you *were* in my game?" asked Matt.

Varl nodded. "I *think* I'm convinced."

Targon laughed. "I guess that's as straight an answer as you're going to get."

Matt began to type in the commands to end the level. Images of Vorgs marching into their spaceships dominated the screen. A menu appeared.

"Is everything okay this time?" asked Targon. "*Are* we all going home?"

Matt smiled. He read out loud, "Congratulations! You have completed Level 3 successfully and finished *Keeper of the Kingdom* on '*novice difficulty*'. Do you wish to try '*expert difficulty*'?"

"No way!" shouted Targon. "Let's quit while we're ahead."

"I guess I'll press *'Exit'* instead of *'Enter'* then," laughed Matt. He looked up at Varl. "It's been nice working with you, sir. I hope that you and Targon both have a safe trip back to Zaul."

"Likewise, my boy."

"Let's all go home," said Matt, pressing *'Exit'*.

The screen turned black. A small box containing a purple X appeared in the center. Matt clicked on the X to end his game. A loud deep laugh echoed in the room and filled Matt with fear. Purple words scrolled across the screen.

"Quitters are not rewarded. You will regret your decision not to continue."

Epilogue

M rs. Hammond placed the last batch of brownies in the oven. She looked at her watch. Matt had been on his computer game far too long. She smiled. It was Saturday morning. No doubt he was hoping that she'd forgotten his two-hour time limit. He'd played his new game for three hours—plenty long enough! She put her oven gloves down and walked determinedly through the dining room to the study.

"Matt, you've been on that game for hours," she said, opening the door. "Time's up. Have you even got dressed yet? Oh, I'm sorry. I didn't realize that Matt had invited a friend over. I didn't hear the doorbell."

"Excuse me?"

"How rude of Matt not to introduce us. Are you new to the neighborhood?"

"Er, yes . . . I guess so."

Mrs. Hammond stared at the straggly-haired boy. He seemed so much younger than Matt and so bewildered by her questions. His eyes were avoiding her gaze. She smiled at him. "I'm Matt's mom. It's nice to meet you."

The boy looked at his feet. "It's nice to meet you, too," he mumbled. "I'm Targon."

Mrs. Hammond tried to control her surprise. Names got more different with every year that passed.

"Targon. That's nice. What did you do to your arm?"

Targon looked down at his sling. "Oh . . . um . . . I leaped off a building running from alien Vorgs."

Mrs. Hammond laughed. She liked Matt's new friend. He had a sense of humor. "Where's Matt?"

"He'd just finished his computer game when I arrived," Targon replied.

"Good. He's probably getting dressed," said Mrs. Hammond.

Targon gulped and muttered, "I hope so!"

About the Author

H. J. Ralles lives in a Dallas suburb with her husband, two teenage sons and a devoted black Labrador. Keeper of the Empire is her fourth novel.

Visit H. J. Ralles at her website:
www.hjralles.com

Also by H.J. Ralles

Keeper of the Kingdom

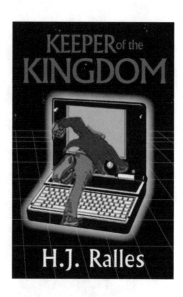

ISBN # 1-929976-03-8 Top Publications January 2001

In 2540AD, the Kingdom of Zaul is an inhospitable world controlled by Cybergon 'Protectors' and ruled by 'The Keeper'. Humans are 'Worker' slaves, eliminated without thought. Thank goodness this is just a computer game – or is it? For Matt, the Kingdom of Zaul becomes all too real when his computer jams and he is sucked into the game. Now he is trapped, hunted by the Protectors and hiding among the Workers to survive. Matt must use his knowledge of computers and technology to free the people of Zaul and return to his own world. *Keeper of the Kingdom* is a gripping tale of technology out of control.

Keeper of the Realm

ISBN: 1-929976-21-6 Top Publications, Ltd.

In 2540 AD, the peaceful realm of Karn, 300 feet below sea level, has been invaded by the evil Noxerans. This beautiful city has become a prison for the Karns who must obey Noxeran regulations or die at their hands. In the second thrilling adventure of the Keeper Series, Matt uncovers the secrets of the underwater world. He must rid the realm of the Noxerans and destroy the Keeper. But winning level two of his game, without obliterating Karn, looks to be an impossible task. Can Matt find the Keeper before it's too late for them all?

Darok 9

ISBN:1-929976-10-0

In 2120 AD, the barren surface of the moon is the only home that three generations of earth's survivors have ever known. Towns, called Daroks, protect inhabitants from the extreme lunar temperatures. But life is harsh. Hank Havard, a young scientist, is secretly perfecting SH33, a drug that eliminates the body's need for water. When his First Quadrant laboratory is attacked, Hank saves his research onto a memory card and runs from the enemy. Aided by Will, his teenaged nephew, and Maddie, Will's computer-wizard classmate, Hank must conceal SH33 from the dreaded Fourth Quadrant. But suddenly Will's life is in danger. Who can Hank trust- and is the enemy really closer to home?

Coming 2005.......

Darok 10

Dr. Gunter Schumann has mysteriously vanished from the lunar colony, Darok 9. Was he kidnapped? And what is the significance of the sinister discovery by scientist Hank Havard and Will, his fourteen-year-old nephew? Determined to solve the mystery, Will and his friend Maddie travel to neighboring Darok 10 in search of the truth. But when Will is captured by a ruthless killer bent on destroying the Daroks, Maddie and Hank are forced to steal military secrets. Can they prevent a lunar war and the destruction of humankind?